D0861515

The Palace
of Wasted
Footsteps

To Martha,

with admiration

and affection,

Cary

September 19, 1998

Stories by

The Palace
of Wasted
Footsteps

C a r y   H o l l a d a y

Cary Holladay

University of Missouri Press
Columbia and London

University of Missouri Press, Columbia, Missouri 65201
Printed and bound in the United States of America
5 4 3 2 1   02 01 00 99 98

Library of Congress Cataloging-in-Publication Data

Holladay, Cary C., 1958–
    The palace of wasted footsteps : stories / by Cary Holladay
        p.   cm.
    ISBN 0-8262-1186-0 (paperback : alk. paper)
    I. Title.
PS3558.034777P35   1998
813'.54—dc21   98-22318
                                                            CIP

☉ This paper meets the requirements of the
American National Standard for Permanence of Paper
for Printed Library Materials, Z39.48, 1984.

Designer: Mindy Shouse
Typesetter: Crane Typesetting
Printer and binder: Thomson-Shore, Inc.
Typefaces: Minion, Berkeley Book

To my father, George Holladay,
and to the memory of my mother,
Catharine Gardner Mitchell Holladay

Contents

The Palace
of Wasted
Footsteps

The Belle Glade

"Well, it *used* to be a nice place," his mother said, stretched out on the bed, drinking tap water from a cup. "Used to be lovely."

They couldn't even get the sea breeze, she pointed out. The windows in their seventh-floor room, overlooking the purple-green blur of Hampton Roads, were sealed shut.

"Let's go for a swim," Eric said.

"Oh, yes!" his mother said. "They have a salt-water pool with lion's head fountains at one end. It's gorgeous."

Eric put on his bathing trunks. His father pressed his nose against the dirty windows, peered down, and said, "That pool's a funny color."

Eric's parents seemed disconcerted, but not necessarily about the pool. Both had just been fired—his mother from her job as a colonial tour guide, for wearing dangly earrings and too much makeup, and his father for growing "progressively unintelligible" (the words of the editor-in-chief, often repeated mockingly by his father) as a journalist.

His mother stayed on the bed, her arm thrown over her eyes, and his father stayed by the window, so Eric went out alone. He had the feeling that they were the only guests on the entire floor. The corridor felt long uninhabited, and the faded paisley carpet sucked up his footsteps. He spotted the ice machine and raised the lid. It smelled sour, and it was empty. He pressed the dark brass bell for the elevator. When after five minutes it hadn't arrived, he took the steps.

It was six o'clock. Usually at this time, his mother would be home from work, her farthingales and flounced costume flung over a chair in her bedroom, while at her upright piano she picked out "Beautiful Dreamer" in single notes. His father would be drinking rum from a teacup ("Let's be civilized about this," he always said as he poured) and watching a game show on TV, taking strong likes and dislikes to the contestants. It had been a long time since their last vacation. Before they were married, his parents had traveled "absolutely everywhere," they told him—the Riviera, Mexico, British Columbia—but always his mother praised the Belle Glade Hotel, where she claimed she had spent her happiest hours as a child. They had all been surprised that it took less than an hour to drive there from Williamsburg. His mother's passion about the place warranted greater distance, more effort.

He reached the subterranean passageway that led dimly outside to the pool and walked into the heavy, humid sunlight. Clouds made goose shapes over the sea. The pool was emerald—slimy and slick. Algae trailed from the surface down to the terrifying bottom, and the safety rope, with its small orange buoys, disappeared into the dark depths as if a drowning victim clutched the other end. The silver lions' heads looked small and chipped, their mouths pursed to whistle, with no water coming out. He confronted his mossy foreshortened reflection, then headed to the patch of beach, just a corner of sand bounded by a cement seawall. A sign said "Danger—No Swimming," but he didn't want to swim. An apple juice bottle stuck out of the sand. A dead creature with feathers and claws gripped a chunk of driftwood. He put his toes in the water and watched the big ships moving out of the harbor, far down the Roads. One blasted its whistle so deep and loud that Eric felt the sound in his spine. He turned and gazed at the dark brick bulk of the Belle Glade, its lightning rods shining like spires.

He was hungry. He pictured the dining room his mother had described—starched white tablecloths, long windows draped with green silk, waiters proffering trays of lobster and ham. He went inside and heard someone hiccupping.

In the passageway, he stopped short, blinded by the

dimness after the sunlight. His plastic flip-flops had rubbed a blister between his toes. Yes, someone was hiccupping close by, in lurching helpless gulps. He moved down the hall, turned a corner, and saw a sign that read "The Teenage Room." The hiccupping came from within.

The cavernous room was dark except for one flaring wall, and as he ventured inside, he smelled something waxy and perfumed. Between hiccups, a girl's voice said, "Do you have any gum?"

The girl stepped out into the weak light. She was fat, he thought, with a short pleated skirt on and fat little breasts. Her mouth looked sore.

"No, but if you drink water from the wrong side of a glass, that'll get rid of 'em," he told her.

"Come here," she said. "Are you a teenager?"

"I'm eleven." He didn't like the insolent smile she directed at his bathing suit.

"I'm thirteen," she said, and before he could move, she seized his hand, pulled him to her chest, and kissed him. Her lips tasted like crayons and felt awful—a blubbery suction. He jerked away with a cry.

"Look what I've done," she said, spinning him by the shoulders so he faced the one well-lit wall. The wallpaper had a funny pattern on it, and moving closer, he saw that it was covered with hundreds of red kissprints. Lipsticks were strewn on the floor like spent firecrackers.

"My day's work," said the girl. "Isn't it pretty?"

It almost was, even though the kissprints didn't reach

all the way to the ceiling. "I looked for a ladder in this damn place, but I couldn't find one," she said. "I'm Greta McGurk."

"You smeared that place." He pointed to a messy spot.

"I was being a vampire. Can I kiss you again? My hiccups are gone." She hopped toward him, her short skirt swinging. He darted away, stepping painfully on a hard lipstick tube. Greta laughed and chased him as he sped down the hallway, until suddenly he reached an open elevator with a crowd of well-dressed people getting off. He looked behind him. Greta was gone.

Only part of the dining room was open. The rest was cordoned off and the furniture covered in sheets. Eric's family was seated beside a window—"At least this one's open," his mother said—with a sill dotted with dead flies. They ordered an elegant meal: tomato aspic, steamship round of beef, peas, and roast potatoes. Then they waited. They were the only ones in the dining room. The waiter seemed angry as he plunked bread and butter plates in front of them. A solemn busboy in a wrinkled white coat swept the floor.

"It wouldn't have done any good if you had just taken them off, Ellen," Eric's father said. "Earrings are your style, and I like your nails bright red. Those colonial babes could've learned something from you."

Eric's mother murmured, "Jody, I don't think it was about jewelry and makeup anyway. Oh, maybe it was!

Maybe I wasn't authentic enough, but I give a good tour. Rita just said I wasn't working out." Rita Ritter was the tour guides' supervisor.

Eric had become aware, at some point, of his mother's beauty, perhaps when men called her at home to say they had been in her tour of the Governor's Palace, and they would be in town for a few days, and, a-hem, could they meet with her? For that reason, she said, she had stopped telling her last name. Still, men waited for her after work. There'd be a gentleman cooling his heels on the back steps of the Palace or the Raleigh Tavern or the Wetherburn or wherever she happened to be working, ready to put out his arm and escort her down Duke of Gloucester Street.

"They want to go back in time," she'd say. "That's what it's all about. Not about *me*. They just think women were more mysterious back then."

A golf pro, visiting Williamsburg for the Kingsmill tournament, would wait beneath the Osage orange tree in the front yard of the Palace, and Eric's mother would talk with him after her shift was over. Eric had seen them laughing together. The golfer was younger than she was, she had reported, "but he says he doesn't care. It's sweet. At least he isn't married, like most of them."

Eric loved to watch his mother teach her groups about flowers and herbs. Grapevines, lavender hedges, and trellises of hops made a suitable background for her. In the garden of the George Wythe house, she pointed to columbine, and as if by magic, hummingbirds appeared in shimmers of jade at her elbow, taking their fill of the sweet red blooms. Eric liked to think about George Wythe, poisoned by his nephew. He liked to talk with his mother about it.

Now Eric's father said, "Rita Ritter's jealous of you. You call *her* boss and get your job back. I want a drink. I'm not too worried about your situation, Ellen. Mine, though." He tried to summon the waiter, who ducked behind a torn Oriental screen.

Eric knew his father's career had once involved world events. He had posted stories from Turkey (where in a knife fight, he said, he received his ear-to-chin white scar), from Burma, and from parts of Africa that now had different names, and all of this was in pursuit of news about war. Then his career had "tamed," as he put it. For the last year or two he had spent most of his time at home on the porch glider, "making himself useful," he would say. With pinking shears, he whacked off old jeans into shorts that pleased everyone in the family. He rearranged the collections of rocks he and Eric's mother had gathered in their travels. To Eric he described an evening in a remote part of British Columbia, "with wild gray waves and blackberries. We saw migrating whales."

Now he said, "What a *demonic* little girl. Was she raised by gypsies?" and he gestured in delight to Greta, who swept into the room and hurried toward a table prepared by the solemn busboy. She had arranged her hair in long thick candle curls. The busboy pulled out a chair for her and she sat down without even a glance in Eric's direction. Eric's father said, "Maybe I was ready to quit anyway. Sending me out to cover a zoo benefit. When I was a war correspondent! Where's our food?"

Greta was being served. They could smell her plate of baked chicken with savory dressing. When she raised her finger, the busboy hurried over and poured her a cup of coffee.

The waiter appeared and slammed a basket of rolls on Eric's table. Eric's father caught the waiter's wrist. "Serve us right," he said. "Where's our supper?"

The waiter jerked his arm away. Eric noticed he was big but young, not a grown man at all. "I thought I worked in a classy place," he said. "I could have worked at Busch Gardens this summer."

Eric's mother was watching Greta. "You'd think her mother wouldn't let her eat all that butter," she whispered to Eric. "Shall I ask her to join us?"

Eric shook his head violently.

Eric's father stood up and motioned for his family to stand, like a preacher raising the congregation for a hymn. "We're going somewhere we can *eat*," he said. "We've been sitting here a solid hour."

As they trooped out, Greta smiled at Eric over her coffee cup.

They got in the car, which was close and stuffy, and drove down Mercury Boulevard to a diner that served fried clams and coleslaw. Eric's mother said, "I want to buy something, Jody. I want a fringed leather jacket. If I can't wear my long skirts anymore, at least I can wear something else that's fun. Can we go to a mall?"

Eric's father mopped up hot sauce with his fried

clams and finished his beer. He didn't seem to hear
about the jacket. "That silversmith who goes for you—
that's the one I don't trust," he said. "Or the guy that
runs the windmill. Even that old man at the Powder
Magazine. Maybe it's better you'll be at home now,
Ellen, away from the troublemakers in our life. It'll be a
new stage in our enchantment." His eyes shone as he
drank another beer.

Eric wondered how his parents could sleep. His
room, adjoining theirs, was so suffocating that at last he
got up and went out in the hallway in his bathrobe. No
lights burned beneath the thresholds of the other doors.
Running lightly down the hall, he whispered the room
numbers: "725, 727, 729." One door was unmarked,
and pushing it open he found a storage chamber, empty
except for steamer trunks banked against the walls and
a beehive in the middle of the floor, like a shipwreck.
Long strips of paper peeled from the walls, and moonlight picked out fallen chunks of window glass. He shut
the door and continued down the hall.

Then he saw two figures near the elevator.

"There he is," came Greta's voice.

He went closer. She was with the busboy, who still
wore his wrinkled white jacket. They sat against the wall
with their legs stretched out.

"Want to help us?" Greta said. "See that mail chute?
There's a letter stuck in it. We're trying to get it out."

"I see it." Intrigued, he studied the thin envelope
trapped in the dusty glass chute.

"It's been in there long's we can remember," the bus-boy said shyly. He spoke into his shoulder. His adam's apple looked too big for his neck.

Eric knocked on the glass. The letter didn't move. He took the sash from his bathrobe and dangled it through the tarnished brass mail slot, but it didn't reach far enough.

"What if you called the post office?" he said. "Have you told the mailman about it?"

Greta said, "They'd take it away. We want it. It might be something important, like a love letter."

"Are you on vacation?" Eric asked her.

She shook back her candle curls. "We live here. This is my brother. Tomorrow, he'll be the diner and I'll be the waitress. That other waiter lied about Busch Gardens. They never offered him a job! We don't like him."

"Where's your parents?" said Eric.

Greta said, "They're dead. Our grandmother owns the place. She lives on the eighth floor, the top floor. She spends all her time reading the dictionary."

The busboy said nervously, "We have to take food to her and her cat. Her cat's real old. It's got palsy." He waggled his arms and legs.

Greta said, "Nana broke her finger and wouldn't go to the doctor, so the finger healed on its own, all crooked. She rode a giant sea turtle one time. And she had herself shipped somewhere in a crate. She did it on a dare. That was long ago, but she still talks about it."

"Can I go see her?" said Eric.

"She wouldn't like that," Greta said.

"Our parents died in a riptide," the busboy volun-
teered. "They couldn't swim very good, and they went
out at night and got carried off."

"Here?" asked Eric.

"Right outside, yeah," Greta said. She twisted a curl
around her fingers. "You can see the spot from the seawall. You can see the riptide, even. It's blacker than the
rest of the water."

Eric said, "I wish you still had them."

"In fact we were looking at the water tonight, at that
spot," Greta said.

Rita Ritter, the woman who had fired his mother,
used to be her confidante. Once Eric had gone to the
George Wythe house at closing time on a rainy December day, when few tourists were about, and chanced
upon his mother and Rita Ritter deep in conversation.
Hanging back in the foyer, he heard his mother
say, "It's like wolf's teeth in my heart," and Rita said,
"You poor thing. I bet you think of nothing else." Eric
heard soft sobs. His mother said, "What if I went with
him? . . . to his tournaments . . ." She broke off. Then
came Rita's nasal tones: ". . . so much younger than
you," and he thought she sounded reproachful and
menacing. Clumping loudly down the hall, he found
the two women arranging waxed fruits and marzipan
on a silver epergne. The dining room smelled of lemon
furniture polish and the pesticide and preservatives that
were sprayed on the baked goods. His mother's lashes
were wet as she greeted him cheerily. Rita Ritter ignored

him and said, "Ellen, don't tell the guests that hailstone story anymore. It isn't true."

His mother looked surprised. "You mean about the colonists gathering hail to make ice cream? Visitors love that story. I always tell it right here in this room."

"Think about it," said Rita. "Even in a big hailstorm, have you ever seen enough ice to even chill a glass of Pepsi? Could you possibly gather enough of it, fast enough, to make ice cream? Gossip like that is pernicious to history—like the notion that people were shorter then."

"Weren't they?" said Eric. His mother stared fearfully at him and then at Rita.

"They were not," said Rita. Her hair was pulled so tightly back that he wondered if she could blink. Her eyes looked malevolent—couldn't his mother see it? A big grease spot decorated her broad bodice. "Revolutionary War records give the height of boys not fully grown. Boys your age!" she flung at Eric. "And we should probably stop saying anything about George Wythe's nephew. That poisoning story could be malarkey too."

"Well, I'm tired," said Eric's mother helplessly. She pulled her fan from her pocket and fanned her face, then Eric's, even though the room was cold. She picked up the straw basket that served as her purse and looked to Eric as if asking him to get her out.

"And Ellen," said Rita Ritter, "as mistress of the manor back then, you might have rosy cheeks, but never rosy nails." Rita tensed her shoulders, drew her arms back, and swung an imaginary golf club over the polished floor.

In the morning, Eric and his parents strolled through the hotel as his mother reminisced: "They used to show movies in the evening, with the French doors open to the moon. Lunch was served on the terrace. A harpist played in the lobby, and a band in the gazebo. There was shuffleboard out by the pool, and croquet. Everybody wore white . . ."

The lobby looked sterile and unpainted, with a single clerk hunkered down at the desk and frizzled palms rearing from cobwebbed corners.

They made their way to ground level. Eric was hungry for breakfast, but his father had vowed they would never again set foot in the dining room.

"Oh, the *Teenage* Room!" his mother cried. "I remember it. I fell in love here once. Nobody says 'fell in love' anymore." She pushed at the door, but it was locked. After a pause she said, "Jody, don't you think I should just call Rita and ask if—"

"You ought to kick that frog-faced busybody in the fanny," said Jody.

From the outside end of the hallway, a small group breezed in, and Eric recognized the well-dressed people he'd seen on the elevator: three couples wearing floppy hats and outfits in shades of magenta and tangerine. They beamed at Eric's parents.

A thickset suntanned woman asked them, "Are you staying here? We're leaving. We're skinny-dippers.

Have you seen that pool?" Her companions made sounds of disgust. A man beside her said, "We're heading to Virginia Beach." He named a hotel. "Join us?" He included Eric in his grin.

Another man slid his hands up his sleeves like a mandarin and snorted. To the first man he said, "You just *watch*. You never even get in the water. You just watch and get drunk."

"Well?" the suntanned woman asked Eric's parents, her lips curving. "Want to come? It'll be a party."

"Sorry, we're unemployed," Jody said and laughed. "Also underage and uninterested. Disinterested, I mean."

They left the skinny-dippers and went outside. The sun hit the sea's horizon hard. A gull pumped by so low that Eric could see the black seed of its pupil. A buoy chimed; the heat of the cement burned through his sandals.

"I was awake all last night," Ellen said, "looking out the windows. The harbor was so pretty. In the dark, the ships' lights looked like a necklace of jewels. What if we'd gone with them, Jody? Who's to say they're not just having fun?" She started to cry.

Eric's father took her in his arms. Fumbling in his pocket, he took out some money and handed it to Eric. "Go get some breakfast," he said. "Anything you want."

The money felt soft in Eric's hot palm. He watched his father lead his mother up on the seawall, their legs white and thin in their denim cut-offs. He wasn't hungry. His parents' voices sounded like the gulls' cries.

He walked all the way around the hotel, but he didn't see any restaurants or coffee shops. At last he went back into the Belle Glade, through the empty dining room and into the kitchen.

Greta and her brother sat on high wooden stools at a long counter. The kitchen was huge, with three stoves and racks of copper pots. Eric couldn't smell any food cooking, but Greta and her brother were making sandwiches. Bologna, cheese, tomatoes, and pickles teetered in tall stacks on blue platters. Greta said, "Don't we have any spinach? We had some last week." She smiled when she saw Eric.

"Are you guys the cooks?" he said.

"The cook quit," Greta said. "This morning he took all the potato chips and got on a boat. It had a pretty flag on it—yellow and green."

"Brazilian, I think," said Greta's brother. "He wanted to go to Brazil. Or Norway. One of those places."

"What do you feed people who are sad?" Eric asked Greta.

"I always drink coffee when I feel bad," she said. "My brother just sucks the grinds. Nana eats bananas. Want some sandwiches?" She put tomatoes and bologna on thick slices of white bread. Solemnly her brother cut them into triangles with a flashing knife.

Eric put his money on the counter. Greta said, "We might leave tomorrow. The ships come so close to the dock, after all. We could go to an island."

"What would your grandmother do?" Eric said.

"We never know what she's going to do next," said

Greta. "She's talking about tearing the hotel down. We wouldn't like that."

"She's talking about condos," the busboy said. "We like that a little better."

"But we still might leave," Greta said and stretched her arms high above her head. "I want to become a great courtesan. I can do that anywhere in the world. But I'll probably just end up being a lawyer. You can keep your money." With her finger she scooped a bit of mustard from a jar and put it on Eric's lips.

He took the plate she handed him and went outside to find his parents. At first he didn't see them, and his heart went wild. He was sure they had jumped off the seawall, or fallen. Then he spotted them under a small peach tree, his mother lying with her head in his father's lap, and he rushed toward them with his gift of sandwiches.

Runaways

THE YEAR I was seventeen, my best friend Nancy Benedict lost her father in a ballooning accident, and I was crazy jealous. It was terrible, yes, of course it was, yet when I thought and thought about it, the disappearing got to mean something else to me, a sort of marvelous secret. His body was never found. Nancy was mystery's daughter, and that gave her an élan that I envied beyond all reason.

What happened was this: he'd gone up by himself against all warnings, even though the weather was fixing to be bad—you could see the big nimbus clouds boiling in the summer sky, and the leaves on the trees were trembling. Sure enough, there was a thunderstorm, a wild one, and Mr. Jack Benedict got caught in it. He always flew high, in that yellow-red-blue balloon; you'd see him floating all around the Charlottesville countryside. He'd follow the path of a road or a river or a valley, then veer off as he pleased and just ride the currents of air. He'd flown everywhere—Kill Devil Hills and the Eastern Shore. He talked about going to the Andes Mountains.

He invited me to go with him the day he died: "When are you going up with me, Kitty?"

"Sometime," I said, feeling shy. I didn't go that day, or ever.

Nancy had been up lots of times. The balloon scared cows and horses, she said, when it cast its moving shadow over them, and the gondola felt bumpy, like it was on wheels. Ballooning didn't impress her; it was just her father's job. My own father was dead, killed long ago in an accident at the quarry, and I didn't remember him at all. And my mother—my mother embarrassed me, with her garden full of strange prickly flowers and her collection of battered gardening smocks.

"The voodoo lady," children yelped as they went past our house. My mother seemed old to me. Yet the more embarrassed I felt about her, the more I loved her. I didn't tell her my secrets, though; I never did; I never told her how much I thought about Mr. Benedict. I just spent all my time at the Benedicts' house.

I pictured him caught in an updraft, his ropes tangled in the clouds, the gondola skewered by zigzags of lightning, the balloon patched with pieces of his shirt. Maybe he got rescued by a great big bird and was leading a new life somewhere else. I was wild with admiration and longing. I loved Mr. Benedict for vanishing like that. Maybe he'd gone to the Andes! Pictures from my geography book sprang to mind, of sharp coral-shadowed cliffs. But after a few weeks, it was like he'd never existed, from the way his family acted. Nancy's mother had plenty of money. She bought a new car and did the living room over, mixing plaids and stripes and florals like the magazines said you could do. It was enough to make you dizzy. The new TV was huge, and Nancy and I watched it for hours.

Nancy would point at a cat food commercial and say, "That cat's wearing eyeliner, I just know it." She didn't want to talk about anything serious. She didn't want to talk about if her dad was still alive.

Nancy and I had been best friends for ten years, ever since the second grade, when her family moved to town. My mother disapproved of Nancy's family, call-ing them nouveau riche. But Nancy seemed to envy *my* life, even though my mother and I didn't have two nickels to clink together. She loved our garden, where my mother grew forgotten things—goatsbeard, aspho-del, madder vine, creeping Charlie—and she raved over my few personal treasures, which included a silver choker I'd inherited from my grandmother and a Painted Desert paperweight I'd found at a yard sale. Layers of different-colored sand made a pattern of pink, orange, red, and white. You had to be careful not to shake it, or the colors would run together.

Nancy's destiny was set: she would go to the all-girls' college that her mother had attended. When Nancy de-spaired of ever having dates, her mother said, "There'll be men teachers. And visiting poets, guys like that. You can screw *them*. I did!"

"Good Lord, Mama," Nancy said, turning red.

Nancy's mother drank champagne all day long and wore halter-top leather minidresses. People thought she was Nancy's sister. Her one widowhood economy was doing her own lawn. She canceled her lawn service and bought hedge clippers, electric shears, an edger, a riding mower, and bags of fertilizer. She'd get the grass in shape and then start on the flowers, she said. She wanted flowers like my mother had. She wanted to grow weird herbs and wear floppy hats. "I'll make pennyroyal tea like your mother does," she said to me, "and lavender jelly."

Nancy and I watched Mrs. Benedict riding the big new mower like it was a bronco. She stuck her legs out, dangling her high heels, and floored that sucker, racing downhill, uphill, round and round the fancy house with its upstairs and downstairs porches, waving to Nancy and me with her plastic wineglass. She got a suntan. She looked great. She didn't seem to miss Mr. Jack Benedict one bit.

Nancy had a spoiled younger brother, Steddy, who was lazy and always talked about cooties. I said, "Steddy, you ought to help your mother with that yard work," and he said, "Not unless I get paid."

I knew he had a big allowance. Even if he got paid, he wouldn't mow the grass. Today, Steddy Benedict's a powerful, rich, shady somebody who owns a lot of property in Charlottesville, and I bet he's still never done any yard work.

Even then, I worried about Nancy. She was too pretty. She already *had* screwed a visiting poet, a frail man who came to our high school and read awful, rhyming stuff about blood and bones. Nancy reported that he wasn't very good. Back then, we were convinced an orgasm could last an hour. We were officially in search of it.

"But what did he *do?*" I said. "I want details." We were in Nancy's room. The quilt on her bed had cost a thousand dollars. They hadn't done it there, of course; the poet had a motel room. Nancy gave me the little wrapped Camay soaps from the motel bathroom. They were so strong-smelling that we both sneezed.

"He did say a nifty thing," Nancy told me. "He said he'd like to scratch my name on a windowpane with a diamond."

Steddy, smirking and eavesdropping in the doorway, said, "That guy came to my class, too. He's got cooties." Nancy threw a boot at him. Steddy was such a little snot. Even when I was so horny I wanted to wrastle just about any boy to the ground, I couldn't stand that Steddy. Yet the poet did look like he'd have cooties, and something about his nose made me think of the word "parsnip," even though I wasn't sure what a parsnip was.

It wasn't the first time I'd been caught up in the life of somebody who had disappeared. All through junior high, it was Amelia Earhart. Nancy humored me in that phase. We'd look at each other and murmur, "Howland Island," which was Amelia's destination, or we'd say in sepulchral tones, "Fred Noonan"—Amelia's copilot— and though Nancy always burst out laughing, my eyes would fill with tears of glorious fright. I collected maps and books and newspaper clippings about Amelia and her Lockheed Electra and her husband, George Putnam, who had given her a gold cigarette case inlaid with rubies, each jewel representing a campfire they'd made on a beach. It was the most romantic thing I could imagine.

Then somebody even better came along: Virginia Dare, the first English baby born in the New World. Her grandfather was Captain John White, who helped set up the settlers' colony on Roanoke Island, way back in fifteen hundred and something. Actually, I had first learned about Virginia Dare in the fourth grade, but I forgot about her until one day when Mama sent me to the grocery store for butter. I picked up a box of Land O'Lakes, and suddenly the Indian maiden on the cover seemed to crane her neck right off that box and say, "Here I am, a white girl dressed up in feathers!" The name *Virginia Dare* popped into my head, and I stopped right there in the grocery store with the butter in my hand, convinced that Virginia Dare had been carried off by the Indians and was raised by them, safe and happy.

So I started collecting history books and arrowheads, and I tried to convince Nancy to go on a bus trip with me to Roanoke Island, North Carolina, but Mama said it was too far for us to go by ourselves. She quashed a trip to the Dismal Swamp, too, where I'd wanted to go to soak up the atmosphere.

The thing was, I was so close to Virginia Dare's life that I could imagine all of it—the pines, the creeks, the thick white dust, the dragonflies and crickets in the corners of the log cabin, the Atlantic horizon where the poor, sick, starving settlers squinted, hoping to see Captain John White's supply boat sailing toward them. After all, he'd been in England for three whole years! When he finally did get back, what did he find but the few little cabins, deserted and wrecked, some rusty armor lying in the sand, and the word "Croatan" carved on a tree. What did Croatan mean, anyway? The teachers and history books were vague about Croatan.

"I bet Virginia Dare turned out perverted," I announced to Nancy one day, back when her father was still around. "How else could she be, after what she'd have seen? People crawling through the palisade with their bodies chock full of arrows! Human porcupines. She'd have been a warped little girl." The thought gave me a weird kind of satisfaction.

Nancy's father tuned in—we were sitting out by their pool—and he said, "Do you girls want to go up with me? Man, what a beautiful Bermuda High." He stretched out his arms to the wide sky.

Nancy's mother said, "Why aren't you over at the Boar's Head Inn right this minute, Johnny? Don't you have some honeymooners to take up?" She was painting her nails; her half-moons were silvery blue, the rest of the nail was pink. It sounds tacky, but really they were beautiful. She and Nancy's father were drinking brandy alexanders. I thought it was snazzy that she called her husband "Johnny" even though everybody else called him "Jack."

"I'm sick of honeymooners," said Mr. Benedict, "but yep, I better get over there and take 'em up."

"I have to go home," I said. "It looks like it's going to rain."

That was the first time he'd ever invited me, and I wanted to go ballooning, I really did. But I wondered why he wasn't afraid of the sharp little breeze that nipped at the tops of the trees. Anybody would know that meant a storm. A stiff rain was falling by the time I got home, and I only lived at the end of the block. I was shocked that Mr. Benedict didn't know more about weather. He was a *safety nitwit,* a term I'd learned in first grade to describe people who walked around holding scissors the wrong way, didn't look before they crossed the street, and grabbed hot things off the stove without a potholder. That day, the first time he invited me, it turned out that he was safe after all. He and the honeymooners didn't launch; they sat in the bar of the Boar's Head Inn having Welsh rarebit and beer.

"Get a boyfriend, Kitty," Nancy's mother told me that summer. "Get your mind onto something important."

But I didn't have a regular boyfriend, and neither did Nancy. Oh, we had dates. We experimented, like with the poet. There just wasn't anybody to be in love with.

So Nancy bemoaned her fate: the girls' college. I was better off—I would go to William and Mary. I could hardly wait.

This was what happened the day Mr. Benedict disappeared: it was Nancy's seventeenth birthday, and unaware of tragedy about to strike, we celebrated. I gave Nancy the Painted Desert paperweight. She wasn't having an actual birthday *party*. Besides me and Steddy, there was only one other guest—a new boy named Paul Faw. He had just moved into town, and all we knew about him was that he was adopted, he stammered, he had asthma, and his doctor had actually prescribed a chihuahua as a cure, heaven knows why. That's still the first question I ask doctors when I meet them (socially, not in their offices): Why a chihuahua for asthma? My mother said the doctor was German, and the right age to have done bad things over in Germany, and that made us feel sorry for both Paul Faw and his little dog. She also said Paul Faw's parents were nouveau riche like Nancy's, but I was beginning to see that that was better than no riche. I've never met any other doctor who's prescribed a chihuahua as a cure for anything at all.

Paul Faw also had a cat, he told us, a pregnant cat. He told Nancy, "You can have one of the kittens; you'll get to choose." I felt a sharp stab of hurt that he didn't offer me a kitten, too. Nancy looked delighted.

Nancy's birthday was the day after the Fourth of July. Her cake had little flags stuck in it, and we lifted out the toothpick flags and sucked the icing off them. It was a day of uncertain light, so that the afternoon air looked green, and the radio excitedly warned of thunderstorms, yet Mr. Benedict was off ballooning. Mrs. Benedict was shopping. Nancy and Steddy and Paul Faw and I sat poolside eating crabmeat canapés left over from Mrs. Benedict's luncheon club and taking turns trying to swim the length of the pool underwater, while Paul Faw exerted a spell over Nancy and me, so that soon we were competing for his attention, swimming faster and faster to get out of the pool and back to the umbrella table where he sat, dressed in plaid trunks but completely dry, forbidden by his doctor to swim.

"I'm to have hypnosis tomorrow," he announced. "My doctor believes it could cure me."

"Wow," I said, before I could catch myself, and Paul Faw dropped his eyes and nibbled his cake.

I'd expected to want to make fun of him behind his back, and instead I was longing to wrastle him to the ground. The chihuahua trembled in his dry embrace, while Nancy cooed and fed it canapés, just managing to brush Paul Faw's arm with her hand. Steddy eyed the dog evilly, gobbling cake, scarfing the sugary red, white, and blue Uncle Sam decoration off the top. I said, "Steddy, you cheapskate, you didn't give your own sister a birthday present."

To which he picked up the Painted Desert paperweight and shook it as hard as you'd shake a bottle of salad dressing, shook it to ruination. I lunged for Steddy's arm, but by then all the colors had run together, and the Painted Desert was just a nondescript little glass container of pink sand. We fought. Somehow, the canapés got knocked over, and Nancy got cake in her hair, and in the melee, Paul Faw said, "Please stop, I beg you!"

I goggled at him, ashamed for how affected he sounded. Here I was, falling in love with him, and he sounded like a damn sissy. The words "I beg you" poisoned the humid air.

"What do you think you are, English or something?" said Steddy. He laughed rudely at Paul Faw.

"Leave him alone, Steddy," said Nancy, who looked as humiliated as I felt, and to save the day, I whipped off the top of my bathing suit, flung it at Paul Faw, and jumped into the pool.

Cold as ice, Paul Faw actually said, "You'd better get out, I just saw lightning."

As if he hadn't even noticed my breasts!

Then Steddy grabbed the chihuahua and tossed it in the water, so it landed near me, fighting for its tiny life, and old Steddy jumped in, too, making a big splash and trying to dunk me. That left Nancy free to make time with Paul Faw. They set the table to rights again and continued eating canapés as if they were grown-ups. It made me so mad. Hailstones big as ping-pong balls plopped into the pool, while lightning forked all around the Benedicts' beautiful lawn. It must've been right then, though we didn't know it, that Mr. Benedict was busy disappearing into the storm.

By now, Mr. Benedict must have circled the globe. He's flown through snow, fireballs, meteor showers.

He's stretched out his hand and touched the hot sparkly tail of a comet, harvested rattly old expired weather satellites for devices that measure the wind. I picture him with wind chimes, tinkly abalone disks strung on dried seaweed, trailing from the wooden gondola where once so many brides and grooms popped the corks on bottles of Korbel. The wind is always with him. I believe he thinks of me.

He has made any number of Great Landings, but always in places where people don't know him, villages so far-flung that the inhabitants would never think to contact the AP wire service, the missing persons' bureau, or certainly Mrs. Benedict, who managed to drop her electric hedge trimmers on her foot and cut off part of her little toe. She promptly started dating the surgeon who sewed it back on, and then she went to a lawyer to find out how soon she'd be "legally free again," as she said briskly; she went out with the lawyer too. Gleefully she told Nancy and me that the lawyer was better looking, but the surgeon was better in bed.

"And he's a wonderful doctor. Why, just this morning, he took somebody's esophagus out!"

"Yeah, and I wonder what he did with it," Nancy said.

Mr. Benedict comes swirling down from the sky, the great balloon swooshing, its dangling ropes as lively as charmed snakes. He survives a rough landing in a Scottish loch and accepts an honorary tartan. He descends into a flutter of bats in the lavender sky of Borneo, sweeps down on a sunglazed beach in the South of

France and dines on three kinds of ices: banana, passionfruit, and mirabelles.

He just can't stay still anymore. He's not homesick for Albemarle County, though sometimes when he sleeps on the worn, scratchy floor of the gondola, he dreams about its rumpled green hills, sees his kidney-shaped blue swimming pool, his daughter Nancy's blonde head.

He can talk with the birds now. He can gaze down into the Pacific and see starfish on the ocean floor. But he just keeps going higher, into that thin, cold air where all you feel is rush and glory and the beat of your heart.

One day a couple came to Nancy's house and told Mrs. Benedict they'd been promised a balloon ride and had come, by golly, to take it.

"We sent the money a long time ago," the man said.

"But my husband's gone. Dead, didn't you hear about that?" said Mrs. Benedict, who by then never even mentioned Mr. Benedict anymore and spent all her time getting ready for a vacation trip with the surgeon; they were going to the Canary Islands. She didn't know where the heck the Canary Islands were, she told me, but film would probably cost more there, so she was stockpiling film and flip-flops, sunblock and sarongs. Her suitcases filled the house, spilling sleek negligees and lacy bustiers. Nancy and I helped her pack while the surgeon sprawled on the sofa popping the plastic bubblewrap that had packaged the mail-order lingerie. He held his stethoscope to Nancy's ears and popped a few bubbles into the sensor, and Nancy jumped.

"Oh, quit it," she said, as if he were Steddy.

"He died in an accident," Mrs. Benedict cheerfully told the couple at the door, "or at least that's what we think. We never found him!"

She smiled and waited for them to go.

The man was short and powerful-looking, and from what I could glimpse in the doorway, as nervous as a jumping bean. He was young, with long hair and wire-rim glasses and a messy mustache. "But I've *got* to go ballooning," he said. "It's a wish of mine, and she—" he jerked his thumb toward the woman at his side—"she's granting my wishes."

By then I was spending more time than ever at Nancy's house, far removed in spirit if not distance from my mother's madder vines and directives. I wondered why Nancy didn't make the most of her position—it was damn glamorous to be the daughter of a vanished balloonist, yet she was vague and dreamy, and mildly rather than grandly sad, a condition I attributed to Paul Faw. We couldn't talk about him—a bad sign— except to discuss his cat's gestation, and what colors we hoped the kittens would be. If Nancy got an hour-long orgasm with Paul Faw, on top of having a disappearing father, I didn't think I could stand it.

So there on the Benedicts' doorstep was this insistent pair of balloon-ride customers, talking about granting wishes. I was intrigued, but Mrs. Benedict just said,

"Find somebody else to take you up. Look in the Yellow Pages!" and she shut the door.

I couldn't help but follow that couple out the door, getting up and floating past Mrs. Benedict as if I'd been loosed from guywires. The couple headed toward a brand-new, top-down convertible and leaped into it without opening the doors. They jumped clumsily and matter-of-factly, as if they'd made an agreement to always get in the car that way. I was fascinated.

"Wait a minute," I said to them.

The man's companion reminded me of the Old Maid in the deck of cards—wan, sly, and abiding, her hair in a bun, her eyes mere dimples behind her glasses. She drummed her fingers on the steering wheel.

They ignored me.

"We could go hang-gliding, Norman," the woman suggested. "Sky-diving, bungee-jumping."

"No, Gabrielle, it just would not be the same," the man said. "Damn it!" He punched the car seat and thrust his fingers through his hair. "For years, I've wanted to go ballooning with Jack Benedict."

"Make another wish," Gabrielle told him. She started the car.

Suddenly, Norman turned to me. "What would *you* do?" he asked me. "Gabrielle and I have decided to live each day as if we'd die tomorrow. We do everything we've ever wanted to do. She grants my wishes, I grant hers."

Gabrielle backed the car out of the driveway, but I

trotted alongside it. Norman said something to Gabrielle, and the car lurched to a stop.

"So what *would* you do?" Norman said.

"I'd go to the Dismal Swamp," I said.

"We did the Dismal already," snapped Gabrielle, frowning at me. I noticed they didn't have on wedding rings, but as Mrs. Benedict always said, that didn't mean a thing. Norman was cute, I decided. And Gabrielle was old enough to be his mother. How much of a rival could she possibly be?

"How about Luray Caverns?" I said.

"Luray Caverns," Norman said to Gabrielle. "Yes, that's a wonderful idea. I've wanted to go there forever!" To me he said, "Want to come along?"

So I got in the car, leaping over the side like they'd done—and off we went.

We did not (as rumor had it) engage in wild sex parties, Norman and Gabrielle and I, although I did travel with them for a week or so, calling my mother now and then to let her know where I was, and to catch up on her garden news. Preoccupied by a leaf-hopper explosion, she didn't seem too upset about my sudden journey.

And it was okay! Norman and Gabrielle were no crazier than they seemed on first impression, and they were rich, so we stayed at nice places and ate what we wanted. At motels, we each had a separate room. I had found the perfect traveling companions.

We did go to Luray Caverns, where Gabrielle burped so loud that it echoed for miles down the cave, and spilled her can of Coke on Norman and me. The guide hissed at us, "Please be quiet so I can play the music!" and during "The Bells of St. Mary's," rendered on stalactites, I started to wonder, What have I done?

"Are you-all bank robbers or anything? Are you married?" I whispered there in the cave, so I would know who I was dealing with.

"We divorced each other," said Norman. "We're transformed."

"He's my goad, I'm his nemesis," Gabrielle said. "We've made a pact to stay together till the new century comes in."

As we drove away, Norman said, "That was wonderful. All those rocks looked like something else. Thank you, Kitty, and thank you, Gabrielle."

Gabrielle took one hand off the steering wheel, squeezed his knee, and said, "We live life on the big screen."

Sometime between our trip to the Charles Town racetrack (which we visited at three o'clock in the morning—that was one of Gabrielle's wishes) and an evening at a circus near Wytheville, I tried to fall in love with Norman. If he'd tried to get me alone and wrastle me to the ground, I'd probably have let him. But he and Gabrielle were wrapped up in each other, or in living as if they were dying, so I said good-bye to them and took a Greyhound bus home. When I walked up the sidewalk to my house, I saw my mother watering her zinnias in the dusk. Sunflowers made a wall of yellow saucers beside the front porch.

"I'm glad you're back," she said, offering me a drink from the hose. "All week I've smelled other people's barbecue smoke, and I think that's the loneliest smell in the world, if you're not invited to eat with them."

I threw my arms around her. Her straw gardening hat pricked my cheek.

"Nancy ran off too, I'll have you know," she said. "With that poet fellow."

"The poet?" I said. "Oh, it can't be true!"

Weeks later, I got a phone call from Nancy. She and the poet were living in Washington, D.C. "The thing was," she said, her voice urgent and faraway, "I kept thinking about what he'd said to me, about scratching my name on a windowpane. It drove me crazy, Kitty, it really did!"

Incredibly, they stayed together, though not for long, because the poet really was frail, and about six months later, he really did die, leaving Nancy with a few boxes of his chapbooks and favorite polka recordings, all of which she placed in a metal foot locker and made Steddy bury in the Benedicts' backyard, "as a time capsule," she said. She was beside herself, hinting that they'd been married, although she didn't have a ring, just a book jacket he'd signed for her that featured a black-and-white photograph of the poet petting a giraffe at the National Zoo. One of the giraffe's ears was cut off at the top of the picture. The poet had on bell-bottom jeans and a leisure suit top.

Two years later, Nancy dropped out of the women's

college and married a tennis pro. He had superstitions about what to wear when he played a match, and what to say as he served the ball, and what he should eat before he played. Nancy bought the tennis pro lots of eighteen-karat gold neck chains and gave cocktail parties at which she served Charlottesville food: pound cake, wine jelly, curried beef dip, and ham biscuits. "Slice that ham just as thin as a bee's wing," she'd tell her caterers. She stayed pretty. She wore the green and white and navy-blue linen dresses that are part of the language of rich Southern women. Her voice changed so that it was like the tennis pro's—like a TV announcer's—but she kept her same laugh. When they were divorced, and the tennis pro got custody of their twins, Nancy started shoplifting things.

"My poet was also a magician, did you know that?" she told me once, when I ran into her in a department store. I had just seen her slip a pair of legwarmers into her pocket, but I didn't say anything; maybe she had cold legs. She looked sad, yet fiercely animated. "A magician," she insisted. "I was his helper. He cut me in two, Kitty, and put me back together. I'm so proud of that," she said.

"I still think about your father," I told her.

"Do you, Kitty?" she asked. "We never heard anything more about him." She fingered the legwarmers nestled in her pocket. "Sometimes when it's windy enough to blow clothes off of clotheslines, I think about him, too."

A few weeks after Mr. Benedict disappeared, Paul Faw's cat gave birth, and since Nancy was off in Washington, that made me, quite naturally, "the godmother," as Paul Faw languidly put it when he phoned me. "So you can come over and choose a kitten, but you can't stay long. I have a party to attend."

Of course I wasn't in love with him anymore! But I did put on extra mascara and a tight pink sundress. With a sophisticated cough, Paul Faw ushered me into his big stucco house, and I knew from the silence that we were alone.

"The kittens are upstairs," he said.

And he led me to his bedroom!

It was furnished in black leather, with track lighting and a thick cream shag rug.

"You've got an ant farm," I said, pleased, leaning over to examine it. The ants had tunneled and burrowed intricately between the glass walls.

"They impressed me at first, but not anymore," said Paul Faw. "Once you see what they do, it's easy. Here's the kittens' new place."

He pointed to a pile of laundry beneath an open window. Three kittens slept there, head to belly, along with the chihuahua.

"Where's the mother cat?" I said.

"Oh, en route," said Paul. "She's moving them up here, from under the porch, because a dog came by this morning and scared her. She climbs up the side of the house and brings one in every so often."

We sat down by the laundry pile. The kittens were long-eared, striped creatures, not quite as cute as I'd hoped. The fat little snoozing chihuahua looked "almost dead," Nancy would say; I could just hear her voice.

"I miss Nancy," I said. "Don't you?"

Paul Faw waved his hand. "She's a fool, Kitty. She's missing an incredible party this afternoon." For a moment I thought he meant us—being with him and me—but he said, "I'd actually invited her myself. It's at a club out on the river. Great big oak trees grow right down to the banks, and their yellow leaves float out on the water. Everybody's going to roast for a while in the sweat lodge, then jump in the river."

"I thought you were too delicate for stuff like that," I said. I wanted to hit him. "Nancy's no fool," I said.

He took my hand and drew me toward the bed, with its black leather headboard and its acre of cream chenille, and he said, "I'm stronger than you think. I've been hypnotized. My asthma's gone!" His breath smelled bad and his eyes crinkled up.

I broke away from him and ran out of the room, down the stairs, and out of the house. I heard Paul Faw laughing at me, a high silly laugh, but I was safe. I turned and watched the mother cat inching up the wall of his house, getting a purchase on the stucco with her stubborn claws, gripping a kitten in her jaws. Step by step, she navigated upward, with such incredible care.

The thing is, as the years go by, I think about Mr. Benedict more and more. "When are you going up with me, Kitty?" he said to me. I like to believe that invitation is still open. One day he'll land in my backyard, right here at the house my mother left to me, and he'll hand me a gold cigarette case etched with a map and studded with rubies, one for every place he's been.

I have become my mother, the flower sorceress. I wear her hats and tend her herbs, and children call me the voodoo lady and think that I am she, though she is gone.

I've been in love so many, many times. I've felt that shift, that turning tide, and the urgency of my thoughts is such that in a car I swerve and weave as I write them down, write notes about the men I've loved, on little scraps of paper as I drive my car. Just this morning I pulled up to a stoplight, and there on the corner, a man and woman kissed and kissed, and the red light went on and on, and I thought I would die right there, from the hurt of it.

Loving Mr. Benedict sustains me in so many ways.

I think he grew up in a poor part of Fauquier County, though he never talked about it. Brilliantine made his black hair crisp and shiny; I remember that. I think about him when a storm's rising, when the edgy summer wind sounds like sugar being poured.

And I have seen him, yes. I've spotted him boarding a train in Philadelphia, eating a funnel cake at the Virginia State Fair—at which times I think, He did it, he passed into another life. So I let him be. My beam of light, my own personal star.

Rapture

I.

O n a day of curtain-fading sun, in the White River Valley of Arkansas, Etta Rockett's mother handed her a clear glass egg and said, "Go put this in the old hen's nest to make her start laying again." The glass egg felt magically cool and smooth in Etta's palm.

So Etta went to the barn. In the dim mote-sifting air, thick with smells of straw and dung, the hen presided, her feathers red-gold, her eyes bright with hatred, like an old woman changed to a critter by some spell, her nest balanced on stacked empty crates. Etta battled her fear of the hen.

The afternoon light was strong, but she was in the barn where it was almost dark. She went close to the nest and stuck out her arm. As the glass egg rolled into the warm straw, the hen speared Etta's hand with her beak. Bright blood spurted from the broken skin, and the frenzied hen spun on her nest. Etta stumbled out of the barn and back to the kitchen where her mother and her aunt were making pies.

"It's awful to think that when you die, your life just *ends*," Aunt Gloria was saying. "Why, Etta, you got pecked."

Etta went to the sink and turned on the faucet. Electric pain ran up her arm. She listened to her mother's dreamy, bossy remarks to Aunt Gloria: "Put some bourbon in the whipping cream, and chop the peaches smaller. Speaking of dying, remember how we wanted to be movie stars so we could ride horses and get married a lot and die on camera? Now I don't even like to go to movies, 'cause I'm not in them and never will be."

Washing her hands, Etta remembered a photograph of her mother and Aunt Gloria as young girls wading in the river. They held their wide white skirts up to their knees as if wringing water out of them. In the picture, her mother looked disgruntled, "mulish," Etta's husband would say years later, but Aunt Gloria looked redeemed, impassioned, angelic. Neither sister had become an actress. They had stayed in Arkansas. Etta's mother had married a farmer; Etta was their only child. Aunt Gloria lived with them. Their lives made a rhythm with the peach trees in the orchard that they harvested to make a living.

Etta's mother was old. Her age was a secret, but even at five, Etta was conscious of her as somebody aged and frail, despite her impressive height and girth. She and Aunt Gloria spent their days cooking and talking

and twisting their hair into spit curls. Etta's mother said
she used to have curly hair, but when Etta was born,
her hair went flat. "This baby stole my curls," she'd tell
people, as she brushed her daughter's thin frizzy hair,
and Etta, guilty, longed to shove the curl-magic back
onto her mother's head the way you'd shove a cream
pie into somebody's face.

Etta dried her hands and put a clean kitchen towel on
the hurt one. Blood soaked into the towel fast, so her
mother wrapped the hand in a cloth bandage. The pies
were finished. Her mother licked a dollop of bourbon
cream from her finger and offered Etta what was left in
the bowl: a sweet, sugary cloud.

Aunt Gloria suggested they put the pies away and go
to a race, all three of them. It was the day that a man was
racing a horse. He had done it before and won, and now
he would try again.

The three of them got in their old Plymouth, drove to
the main road, and headed farther out into the country,
to a colored high school. Etta's mother parked the car on
a hard-packed dirt field. A restless crowd sweated beneath the sun. Etta's hand throbbed; the gummy blood
on the bandage smelled bad to her. People had a giddy
look about them. A woman was selling cold drinks from
her car. Aunt Gloria bought a Coke and got hiccups.

"Rub your earlobes; that'll get rid of hiccups," Etta's
mother told her. Etta followed her mother's big hiney as
they edged through the crowd. A rough track was laid
out on the athletic field. They managed to get seats on
the flimsy bleachers, which bucked and swayed so

much that Etta was afraid she would fall between the spaces.

Shading her eyes, she looked out to the track. There were the racers, getting ready: a powerful black man, stretching his arms and legs, and a chestnut stallion jerking its head this way and that. Etta felt scared for both of them, as if whichever lost the race would die. An excited old woman sitting beside Etta told her the names of the racers: "That man there is Floyd, and the horse is named Resolute."

Somebody fired a gun, and the man and the horse sprinted down the field, close together, the man's jaw sticking out ahead of his body as if a magnet pulled him, the horse's sharp hooves dancing, its mane snapping like a dark sail. The red dust they kicked up dissolved before Etta's eyes like a stain. All around her, people cheered and hallooed. Her mother and Aunt Gloria scrambled to their feet, so Etta stood too. It was the man who crossed the finish line first, to wild shouts and applause, and a second later the horse crossed. Victorious, Floyd raised his arms above his head as he kept on running around the track, slower now. The horse trotted smartly; a man caught it by the bridle and swung himself onto its back.

"Floyd won," Aunt Gloria cried, hopping up and down. "Hooray!"

"Look, they've got him up on their shoulders," Etta's mother said, pointing across the jostling crowd to where Floyd rode high. Etta noticed her mother's chin still had a smudge of whipped cream on it.

"Well, let's go on home," her mother said, and they climbed down off the bleachers. The whole thing hadn't taken but a few minutes. Dizzy, Etta felt solid ground under her feet again.

Then she got sick on the grass. Pain seared her hand, the hen's beak a hot poker in the skin and bones, and she choked and shook as she vomited. Aunt Gloria didn't seem to notice; she was caught up in celebrating. She said, "Come on, Sister, let's go speak to Floyd."

"My land, this child's really sick," Etta's mother said. She knelt down and caught her daughter by the arm. "Do you need a doctor?" She put her hands trumpet-fashion to her mouth and cried into the crowd, "Is there a doctor here?" and when nobody came, she and Aunt Gloria put Etta in the car and headed home. Through the car window, Etta saw the horse, Resolute, charging breakneck into the hazy sun. Delirious, she thought the horse followed them all the way home, in long canter-ing strides as if he were swimming in the air.

For a week, Etta fought a fever, and coming out of it, she possessed a strange power, which she discovered one day while sitting out in the yard, under a persim-mon tree. She crooked her little finger to see how many lines it made—to see how many children she would have someday—and a sparrow on the branch above her came fluttering down and alighted on her hand. Its live avian feet felt like wiry fingers; with wonder she exam-ined the bits of purple and pink, even yellow, in its gray feathers. Off it went, launching matter-of-factly into the air. Etta spotted a female cardinal, dull green with a clever pointed head. Raising her hand, she crooked her finger, and the cardinal swooped down and settled on her hand unsteadily, for it was a big bird. The stove-warmth of its body was lovely on her skin.

The newspaper did a story on her, and for a couple of years she was a sensation: Etta Rockett, the Bird Girl. At school, the teacher had to seat her away from the window so that she wouldn't lure birds into the classroom. It all stopped when Etta was about seven, a gift taken away as abruptly as it had been given, around the time her mother died. The birds just stopped coming, no matter if she crooked her finger at them all day long.

She felt forsaken.

"I think it's just a story you tell, to draw people near to you," said her boyfriend years later, the man who became her husband, who liked very much to be near her.

"It was real," she said, remembering the orioles, the tanagers, the mockingbirds that had perched on her hand. "I'll show you those newspaper clippings to prove it. Besides, lots of people remember."

But she couldn't find the clippings, and she felt funny asking people to stick up for her, to insist that what she said was true, so she just turned the memory over in her mind and rolled her eyes when her husband teased her.

Aunt Gloria had finished raising her. Aunt Gloria had married Etta's father, stepping into her dead sister's place as easily as she might have helped her set the table, and the three of them—Mr. Rockett, Aunt Gloria, and Etta—ran the peach farm until the state of Arkansas decided to dam up the White River and turn part of the valley into a great big lake.

The government bought up all the land for miles around. Nobody could tell them no, though one of the Rocketts' neighbors chained himself to his door in defiance and stayed on until the water was nearly to his front steps. Etta's father gave up the peach farm and moved the family to nearby Eureka Springs, where they were close enough to keep an eye on the progress of the lake as it filled, over a two-year period, with the cold clear water of the White River. The mountains all around the lake gave it a pretty shape. Developers laid out fancy neighborhoods and went bankrupt when nobody moved in but eagles and deer. The land went back into wilderness, while the beautiful lake lapped hungrily at the mountains all around it. Sometimes a few dark-tanned, bullet-headed teenagers roared grimly around on Jet-Skis, but mostly the huge lake was empty and quiet.

"It's two hundred feet deep, in places," said Etta's father in awe and sadness, for he hadn't wanted to leave his orchard, and now, running a store in Eureka Springs that sold sachet and dolls to tourists, he was a lost man. With shy pride, he said, "Divers who work on the dam say they've seen catfish that must weigh eight or nine hundred pounds. Man-eaters."

"Oh my," Etta murmured, picturing their peach orchard in crystalline clarity, flourishing underwater, with bream swimming among the branches of the trees and mermaids eating the furry golden fruit. Homesick, she dreamed about the orchard as she lounged at the counter of her father's store, growing up; she sneezed from the sachet and potpourri that tourists bought by the pound. Tourists loved that sachet, even though it was just ground-up dried petals from somewhere else, not Ozark roses at all. The marmalade and pepper jelly in the jars with gingham on top had been packaged in New Jersey; the cornshuck dolls were made in Mexico.

Her father fell in love with the lake. He collected its stories and passed them on to Etta. Most of the tales were sad ones, so that she grew to associate the lake with the urgent tones of her father's voice as he told her about a man who dove too deep and died of the bends, and of a woman who floored her car right into the lake and sank.

"Daddy, I have heard enough," Etta said and put her hands over her ears.

Perplexed, obsessed, her father stood behind her while she helped a customer pick out a hooked rug. To Etta and the customer both, he went on, "Divers sometimes go crazy down there. There's something called the rapture of the deep that's like being drunk underwater, I hear. Nitrogen narcosis. People laugh, they try to talk underwater, they rip off their face masks, they drown."

The customer, an impatient old lady, asked Etta, "Don't any of these rugs come in purple?" and Etta, flipping through the stack of carpets, could not tune out her father's story or turn off the picture in her mind, of a misbegotten diver going down too far. She missed the peach farm. She missed her mother. She had not wanted to move away from the farm. She did not realize how deeply those facts had etched themselves upon her.

II.

Dived, dove, diven, divine: restless, Etta at eighteen looked around for love and lit on a karate instructor named Dana Pentecost. She told her father and Aunt Gloria that the martial arts might save their lives someday. She called the number of the studio—253-KICK— signed up for lessons, and showed up early. "A girl has got to protect herself," she said. Dana Pentecost's tongue lolled out of his mouth at the sight of Etta's hourglass figure and the curves she made as she clenched her fists and made as if to deck him.

"I'm such a bad, bad man," said Dana Pentecost, pinning Etta's arms behind her back as gently as folding butterfly wings. He was a small strong man; Etta could almost have scooped him up in her arms. He was tough and good-looking, with black hair ragged past his ears and a laugh that hovered in his throat. His mouth tasted like olives and sweet smoke. There in his studio, with the rubber mats on the floor that smelled feety and old, and with mirrors all around so you could see yourself prance, Dana and Etta kissed until the rest of his students showed up, smirking to see the teacher caught in a smooch.

When Dana and Etta decided to get married, Etta was proud that Dana announced it to the whole Tuesday evening class. Etta didn't flaunt her garnet engagement ring, but some of the other women were so jealous, a bunch of them quit that night and never came back.

For their wedding day picture, Mr. and Mrs. Dana Pentecost posed at Ye Old Victorian Photography Shoppe in old-timey clothes: a coat and tails for him, a lace jabot and kolinsky shawl for her. Honeymooners from the Missouri Bootheel all the way to the Florida Panhandle had worn those same clothes, jerked from the photographer's wobbly hat rack. Etta treasured the picture. The kolinskies' gleaming eyes kept vigil on her white neck, there in the sepia photograph. How soft their fur had been! She hung the picture next to the photograph of her mother and Aunt Gloria wading in the White River, back when they were young girls longing to be actresses.

"You have married a dangerous loon," said Aunt Gloria, as she and Etta swept the floor of the gift shop and Etta stared at the clock on the wall, mad to get home to Dana, to their apartment over his karate studio.

"He's got charisma," said Etta, squeezing her legs tight together and dabbing green-apple perfume on her neck, "and he's making money. We're saving up to go live in Memphis or Little Rock. He'll open a bigger studio there."

Aunt Gloria piled key rings and packets of peanut brittle on the counter, beside the cash register. *She looks like Mama now,* Etta thought, *so stout and plain,* and she missed her mother as Aunt Gloria said, "I pray for you, Etta, and for your husband too."

Etta loved being a wild man's bride. She got pregnant right away, and she and Dana were thrilled.

Then Dana started fooling with guns, and he turned into a William Tell. After hours, when karate lessons were over for the day, he took to shooting bottles off people's heads. Bottles and apples, peaches and hats—anything that would balance on a head. About his charisma, Etta was right: men and boys and even some hard-ass girls, who loved him like Etta did and who hated Etta for being married to him, begged Dana to shoot between their fingers or to plug a beer can balanced on their stiff-held heads. They played the games outside, on the broken concrete patio behind the studio, with moonlight shining on Dana's gun.

Etta pleaded with him to stop. She always fled when he started shooting. She heard his friends laughing as she ran away to hide upstairs, heard shots rattle out in the soft air of Eureka Springs, and Dana just chuckled at a fat old cop who showed up one evening too flustered to do anything but shake a pair of rusty handcuffs and yell at Dana to knock it off.

Etta was in bed, the covers over her head, when Dana came in that night, out of breath and happy. The cop had broken up the party, but there would be other parties. Dana saw years of fine aim ahead of him, and he could no more cease than a gambler could give up cards.

"I shot a kid's earring off," he said, pulling up the blankets and finding Etta's lips with his own. "I parted a gal's hair."

Etta could just make out his eyes, midnight blue and all delight. She crouched beneath the covers, too furious to reach for him or to back away.

He groaned, "Etta, you light a fire in my fireplace. Come on and devil me, devil me like an egg."

"Do you love me more than them?" she asked him, meaning—your karate students and the rest of the world.

"They don't know me like you do. I'm just a wind that blows through them," he said, and she wrapped herself around him.

The sheriff knew all about William Tell, of course, all about the shooting, and did not do a thing. He was a friend of Dana's. The cop with the cuffs was of no more consequence than a fly, and he never came back.

"You'll blast somebody in the face some night," Etta warned her husband, "and kill them. That's what it would take to make you stop."

But all he shot was his own left foot, as he spun the pistol in his fingers on a night when his luck ran out. Doctors cut off what was left of it, so he was a one-footed man.

"Showing off for your little girlfriends," Etta cried, "and your hero-worshiping boys."

"Leave me alone," Dana said. He gimped around on crutches for awhile. By the time their baby was born, he was back at work giving chop-chop lessons, a twinkle-toes light as air on a good fake foot.

Etta named their tiny daughter Yetive, a beautiful name she'd read in a book. "It rhymes with native," she liked to say. Yetive loved to be kissed and caressed. She mewed for Etta to tickle her little arms with gentle strokes of her fingernails. Heaven, thought Etta, was watching a summer storm from the safe balcony of their apartment, with Dana beside her and Yetive on her lap.

Dana said he would buy their baby a savings bond. Instead he spent lots of money on brand new shoes, several pairs: wingtips, sneakers, bedroom slippers, cowboy boots.

"Derned if I need my old shoes now," he said and laughed. One by one, he threw the old shoes up into the backyard hickory tree. The shoes hung there like fruit, cupping sleet in wintertime, making homes for small birds' nests come spring.

Plump since pregnancy, Etta didn't like the tight binding way her clothes felt, or the sweat on her upper lip that came from her solid weight. So she went on a diet, giving up the crullers and creme horns she adored and becoming very thin, with more energy even than Dana had. *Here we are, a family,* she thought as she blazed through her housework, hearing through the floor of the apartment the stereo that Dana played while he instructed, vicious bass from a scratchy old tape, sounds that would madden the kindest spirit into kicking somebody in the head.

Aunt Gloria died of a stroke, sitting down hard in the gift shop one day on top of a box of wind chimes and dying to the tune of breaking glass. She was buried in a flat rocky cemetery, where plastic flowers wreathed the graves, blossoms all sun-bleached to sad salmon-pink and faint-hearted hazel.

Etta missed them both, Aunt Gloria and her mother. She missed the peach farm and hated the state government for damming up the river and making the big stupid lake.

"I can go back to our peach farm any time I want, in memory," she told Dana. She recalled her sweet room where in the darkness a lost firefly might seek its reflection in the mirror like a beloved. Her hands itched as if from peach fuzz, that gold-dust of her childhood. She used to scoop it up from the troughs in a shed where the peaches were graded, de-fuzzed, and washed.

She remembered a farm next door, and a slow train that moved through the cornfields, the engine a quiet considerate locomotive that didn't want to disturb anybody. She missed all of it. Aunt Gloria's death brought it all back.

She tried to describe it to Dana one morning as he strapped on his artificial foot. "That last day," she said, "the day that Daddy and Aunt Gloria and I closed up the house and left it, was a sunny day, so quiet and still. Crows circled in the sky, and wood smoke rose straight up from the chimney. It was early fall. I wanted to take everything with us, but Aunt Gloria said we'd get lots of new things in town. She even left some furniture behind, like her dresser with the dresser scarf still on it. Daddy didn't try to change her mind."

"Some people had their houses moved," Dana said, pushing up from his chair and springing on his toes.

"Pried up by the foundations and moved away on a big truck. Y'all could have done that."

"I know, I know," she said, "but we just went out and closed the door. Once the lake filled up, the house and all that stuff we left behind must have floated away." Regret panged through her for that time, those things, her family. She remembered a pair of breeze-filled sheer curtains that her mother had embroidered with yellow nasturtiums, and she wept.

"Stupid not to take that stuff, or sell it," Dana said.

"It wasn't like we were rich, either," Etta said.

Dana shrugged and went downstairs to rev up for the karate lessons. The words *bump-toed fool* crossed Etta's mind, a treachery she forced down in her heart as she made the bed, changed the baby, and worked all day at her father's shop. *A jester in my life,* she thought, for Dana didn't much sympathize, he just caught you off-balance. Karate and kissing, that's what he was good at.

She wasn't prepared for Dana to die, to pass away a young man of only twenty-eight, which he did just a few months after Aunt Gloria's stroke: Dana's heart gave out during lessons one night. He spun a student-lady over on her back, as if they were dancing, bending over for a dip, only he went down and never got up again.

Widowed, Etta lost her baby too. Little Yetive got meningitis. Stiff limbs, stiff neck, red spots six inches across, and then she was gone, buried beside her father in the flat graveyard where young trees struggled to bear the weight of winter's ice on their every twig.

It was March, cold and bare, with pipes freezing and

bursting all over Eureka Springs during a late snowfall. Daffodils, pushing up from their snug bulbs, got squelched by sleet. Etta worked like a clock in her father's shop. It was months till she could speak. She held herself together, staving off comfort, turning away from neighbors' pity and customers' chat, putting herself together again from the inside out. She couldn't cry. Mourning, her face looked angry all the time, or like a person finding a way through fog, and she was so complete that she was empty.

She fought forgetting. She feared the time when Dana's fierce karate sneer might recede from her mind, when Yetive's soft remembered weight grew lighter in her arms—a shade, ghost, ash.

She didn't want to see anybody. Against her better instincts, she accepted, after months of importunities, an invitation from a famous judge known throughout the state for signing all documents, even death warrants, with a smiley face. Over dinner, Judge O'Reardan turned out to be a farting, cackling presence. In candlelight, over grilled swordfish, his nose hair looked as long and white as fishing line, and when he drove her home he went the long way, around the lake. He pulled the car over and grabbed at her breasts, his hands cold and busy-fingered, his breath bitter and chalky from the antacid tablets he chewed. Etta's body was a treasure trove, and the judge's limbs were skunks grabbling through it. With improvised karate, Etta fought him off, leaving him pretzeled against the steering wheel so that he honked the horn with his chin.

She slipped out of his Cadillac and crept down to the shore of the lake, gravel and sand sifting into her shoes. The lake stretched out before her, vast and black as the ocean. She remembered her father's stories about giant catfish, desperate divers, and the woman who had floored her car and driven right into the lake. Stars gleamed in pinpoints on the water, as if they had fallen into it. Or maybe the bright spots were peaches from her family's orchard, peaches floating to the surface and bobbing on the mild tide. Etta's mouth watered; a peach was what she needed.

Slipping off her shoes, she stepped into the lake's welcoming edge. Oh, how cold the water felt, and glorious. She waded farther and farther out, her dress clinging to her legs and waist. Her mother and her aunt had wanted to be actresses; they had forded some shallow part of the White River, wringing out their long white skirts. Etta plunged across the shining blackness, her arms chopping the icy water in a hard fast crawl.

Seal-like, she held her breath and dove. Oh yes! She was strong enough to go for miles; her lungs held air enough to get her home, back to the peach farm that was surely close to her now. Her body was a ripple, a current, and without surprise she found herself in the orchard, the treetops brushing her body, and it was spring and harvest time all at once, she saw with joy; blossoms and round gold peaches fell into her hands when she shook the branches. Why, there hung Dana's shoes on the boughs, wingtip and sneaker, which he'd tossed into some other trees a million years ago, behind the karate studio. Yetive needed soothing, wanted her small arms tickled. First, Etta would eat this peach. Her mother was calling her, and the birds came swooping down around her. She wasn't even crooking her finger, yet the birds flew down from the trees. She wanted to eat this sweet gold fruit, but the water was making her limbs slack and heavy, and she couldn't quite bring the peach to her lips.

As the nitrogen bubbles built up their secrets in her blood, her mouth twisted in a laugh, a kiss, and water rushed in to choke her, but she only tasted the ripe sweet peach, which, with an effort, she'd gotten between her teeth. Its fuzzy skin tickled her tongue. She loved it here. She was home, and the slow train was whistling through the neighbors' fields.

But the birds were bearing her up with their wings, and her mother was calling her. Her mother and Aunt Gloria were making pies, and Etta could have some whipped cream if she wanted it. She was rushing through some long tunnel, her arms pinwheeling, the burning stars making sparks in her head. She shot to the water's surface and burst through to the air.

Dawn found her dazed on the coarse sandy beach. She opened her eyes and saw sky and pines. She blinked. A huge fiery cloud passed over, its bottom ragged like that of a great furry cat. Her hair and clothes were drenched and swirly with water. A sound reached her from far away: the judge's stuck horn, a battle cry issuing from the hilly fastnesses above the lake.

Etta pulled herself up. She was very happy. Yes, she

could stand, she could walk. She trudged up the hill to the judge's car. Tossing her wet hair, she peered in and saw him snoring, his lips puffing out with every exhalation. She set out on the road back to town, her soppy dress flapping in the morning breeze, her bare heels growling smartly on the graveled berm.

III.

She closed up the karate studio, packed a suitcase, and went to Hot Springs. At one of the spas, she got a job as a bath attendant. Helping patrons into vats of steaming, bubbling mineral water, she rubbed their skins to pinkness with the rough loofah in her hand.

"Feels like hot 7-Up, doesn't it," she said, unfazed by the sight of belly, breasts, and bush.

She tired of people fast these days. It was always a relief to pull the plug, to help the bather from the bath, clap a terrycloth towel around her, and send her on to hot packs, steam cabinet, needle shower, and massage. The bathers were menaces to Etta's grief. She knew they liked the masseuse better than they liked her; the masseuse was more convivial and never clammed up. Off went the bathers from the luxury spa, soothed and greased, their asses well goosed, their shoulders flexed, their skins smoothed and soles buffed, their lives unchanged by the thin young woman with the loofah in her hand who exhorted them to relax in the deep old clawfoot tub.

I am aging fast as a dog, Etta thought, *seven years for every year I live.* She was twenty-two and a half years old. She felt old and superior to the honeymooners who came to Hot Springs from Cape Girardeau and Pine Bluff and St. Louis. She called her father and told him she would stay in Hot Springs for longer. She liked the smell of the water, the metallic mineral scent that floated always in the air.

Her father sounded kind and faraway. Etta hung up desperate, missing her mother, her mother who sang "Jack of Diamonds" and called snakes serpents. Her mother belonged to an old-timey world, and Etta had thrilled to her stories: as a child, Etta's mother had ridden on the backs of oxen as they hauled timber out of the Arkansas woods; she used to bang her knuckles on a tin pan to fool a swarm of bees into losing their queen and hiving nearby. But Etta had been home; she had heard her mother calling her. Her time in the lake was something she hugged close, a visit she'd stolen from grief itself. And she remembered the day her mother took her to see that man, Floyd, who had outrun the horse named Resolute, and the memory put some hope in her marrow. Her nerves were power lines hung with icicles. She loofahed hard, rubbing the bathers till they squealed and drew away from her, their eyes terrible with indignation.

"Please, Etta, you have got to pamper them; they're our guests," said Ted Stout, the spa manager, who loved her. No matter how many people complained, he would not fire her; Etta knew this and was cool to him, to torment him. He wasn't Dana. She knew she could drown people all day long, and Ted Stout would still greet her with delight every morning and tenderly say good-bye at night, when they were the last two left in the bathhouse.

"My hands get so shriveled," she said at the end of a long wet day, a day when a customer had slipped on the white tiles of the bathing room and injured a toe, blaming Etta for the accident just by proximity. Ted Stout had championed Etta: it wasn't her fault, he said, counting out money to compensate for the lame toe.

Now he flew to find Etta some lotion for her chapped hands. A wishbone of a man, he was, too stooped and melancholy to woo her, so slight that Etta imagined him eating meals of dust. Her allegiances to Dana and Yetive were a moat he couldn't get across.

"Would you like to go to dinner with me?" he asked, sorting loofahs and Lost and Founds under the atomic glare of the fluorescent light, there in the foyer of the bathhouse. "There's a new restaurant where we can get knockwurst and beer."

Who knew but that Ted Stout might be another Judge O'Reardan, fit only for honking the horn with his chin? She rubbed lotion on her fingers, around her garnet ring, as she turned him down: "I do not date. Thank you just the same."

Ted Stout looked sad and then he rallied, holding up something shiny from the Lost and Found box. "Look at this," he said. "A paperweight?"

"Oh!" Etta cried, for in Ted's hand was a clear glass egg just like the one she had long ago slipped underneath the troublesome hen. She told Ted Stout all about

it as she rolled the glass egg over and over in her palm—
about the hen attacking her, about the man named
Floyd who'd raced the horse, about her illness and her
brief ability to charm any bird just by crooking her
finger.

"Do you suppose this glass egg could be the same
one?" she said. "Could the river have washed it out of
my old house and up onto the bank, where somebody
found it?" She shook all over, clutching the glass egg.
Ted Stout stared at her, amazed, and at last he went to
the soda machine and got her a Dr. Pepper. Her hand
trembled as she took the cold bottle from him. She
could hear her Aunt Gloria saying, "Why Etta, you got
pecked."

She wrapped the glass egg in a handkerchief, carried
it home with her, and put it on her dresser beside the
picture of her and Dana in their old-fashioned wedding
clothes. For the first time since Yetive had died, Etta
wept, her heart hurting all out of proportion to something so small and plain, which she had never known
she missed.

Yet in the morning, she got up and walked to work.
Mule-drawn tourist carts, garlanded with flowers,
clattered past her in the sunlight. Tourists waved. To
her surprise, her hand flew up; she was waving back.
She bought shaved ice from a vendor and ate it for
breakfast.

Doll

Boyd found her at the dump—a discarded mannequin. She lay atop a high heap of trash, one foot tangled in an electrical cord, her graceful arms embracing a junked stereo, her earless plastic skull tuned to faraway songs. She was so pretty. He put her in his truck and drove away with her.

On the way home he stopped at a wig shop to buy some hair for her. The door tinkled as he pushed it open. A woman at the cash register was braiding a purple fall, which rested on a Styrofoam model of a head. She said, "May I help you?" without looking up, her fingers busy with the braid.

The shop was dusty. Boyd sneezed. "I'd like to buy that blonde curly wig in the window."

"Go ahead and get it out."

He was annoyed. "I didn't know this was a self-service place."

"If I stop now, I'll lose the pattern, and this is a French braid, hard to do."

He put some money on the cash register. "Who comes in here?" he asked.

"Guys like you, getting a wig for a woman who'd be perfect if she just had curly blonde hair."

Her smile was tight, like a cat's yawn; she had a teenager's freckles but she was about thirty, he guessed. Her own hair was short and spiked. He didn't trust her. He took the wig and left.

The mannequin was propped up in the passenger seat, her painted eyes staring far off as if reading distant signs. Somehow her feathery eyelashes had survived, and her blue eyeshadow. As Boyd drove home, the mannequin felt like company, and it was a good feeling, because he'd been lonely since breaking up with Sandra, his girlfriend of three years. Incredibly, they had even made love as they said good-bye. Afterward, though, he wanted her to leave. And Sandra had been in a hurry to go, ducking out the door with her nurse uniform only halfway on.

So he was surprised to find Sandra in the yard when he got home. It was Saturday; she was usually on duty at the hospital. He hadn't seen her for weeks. Her hair looked grayer and kinkier at the temples and longer in the back.

He swung the mannequin onto the clover of the yard and turned on the garden hose. Sandra laughed.

"Who's this? You didn't waste any time finding somebody new," she said. She knelt to massage the mannequin's hands as Boyd hosed dirt off the palms. A golden fluff of dandelion sprang up between the mannequin's legs; an ant explored a plastic nipple.

"She's just so sweet-looking," he said. "I found her at the dump."

"What are you going to do with her?"

"Name her." He turned the mannequin over as gently as he'd seen Sandra turn a patient in a bed. Her clean white back shone in the sun.

"Elvira," said Sandra. "Ernestine. Zelda."

"Those are ugly names. She has to have a pretty one."

"She had a narrow escape. Do you know that, girl?" Sandra touched the mannequin's cheek.

Boyd played the water over the legs, a final rinse.

"I tried calling you," Sandra said. "I let it ring about a thousand times."

He turned off the hose and stood the mannequin up. The slanted feet wouldn't support her, so he held her around the waist. He had the feeling that at any moment she might start waltzing. Sandra regarded the two of them formally, as if greeting a married couple.

"Don't you want to know why I'm here?" she asked, shading her eyes against the sun. He noticed the wrinkles around her eyes and lips. "I'm pregnant. While you're thinking up names for the mannequin, you might hit on one for the baby."

If the mannequin in his arms had begun to do cartwheels, he would not have been more shocked. "A baby, Sandra?"

"It must have happened that last time. Oh Boyd, I'm

not asking you to marry me." She toed the wet grass with her white nurse shoe. "I can't stay long, I'll be late for work."

"Do you feel all right, Sandra?"

"I'm fine. I want to have it and raise it." She touched his hand. "Do you need to sit down, Boyd?"

He shook his head. "I can give you some money."

From her purse she took out a piece of paper. "How about just a few things I'll need."

Dazed, he read the short list: antique cradle, receiving blanket, antique high chair, shoes in different sizes. He shook his head as if to clear his eyes.

"Don't worry about that stuff," Sandra said. She took his hand and led him into his house. His living room smelled of the pork chops he'd burned the night before. His knees felt loose. He laid the mannequin on the sofa and sat down heavily beside it. Sandra bent down and spread her hands to measure the mannequin's waist.

"Size six," she said, "like I used to be. Oh, Boyd, you're so pale."

She leaned down and kissed his cheek. He reached out and held her face between his hands.

"Sandra." His voice was thick.

She lifted his hands away, her touch light and professional. "I have to go. I've got an old lady on my floor who raises holy heck if I'm late to take her temperature." She brought him a glass of water and then she left.

Later he called her at work and said, "We should get married. All I can think about is how nice you are."

"You're sweet, Boyd, but no." She sounded preoccupied. He heard the hospital intercom in the
background.

"Do you really want to be a single mother?"

"The word 'scandal' has crossed my mind," she said.
"Boyd, all I know is I want this child. I didn't think I'd
get pregnant that last time." She paused. "I'm a nurse
and all. I should have thought. I promise I'll share the
baby with you."

"I'll find you the best damn antique cradle in the
world," he said, and hung up and cried.

He called his mother and told her everything. She
snorted when he told her about Sandra's list.

"A cradle and a bed now, and God knows what-all
later. She'll bleed you dry about this baby, and it could
be somebody else's, have you thought about that? Didn't
she used to date a Polish fellow who worked at a carnival and ate grapefruit with the peel still on?"

"Ma, that was years ago. How do you remember stuff
like that?"

"She told me they'd dated in high school. She
might've gotten back together with him."

He was sorry he had confided in her. She'd never
liked Sandra anyway.

"Well, you'll get a grandchild," he said.

"I've never cared about grandkids," his mother said.
"I'll just worry about this one, like I worry about you
and your sister—your sister who lives in Alaska and
goes to movies by herself. She says she goes with friends,

but I don't believe her. And you aren't cut out to be a policeman at all, but you make yourself be one, and why? To be tough?"

"Sandra's glad about the baby," Boyd said.

"She'll look funny with that baby. People will think she's the grandmother, not the mother."

"Don't tell anybody about this, Ma."

He pictured his mother throwing her hands up in the air. "There's no such thing as a secret, son. It's out."

He often dreamed about the baptism he'd had when he was five. The preacher had led a group of people into the James River. It was an overcast summer day, and Boyd kept waiting for God to knock the thunderclouds aside and speak to the penitents as they crept into the brown water, the women holding their dresses above their knees and wiping their eyes with handkerchiefs as they wept for joy, the men plunging in boldly and becoming short and mysterious as they sank up to their shins in riverbottom mud, their arms resting on the water's surface as if on a table. Boyd held his mother's hand until the preacher took him and lifted him high above the water.

Then the dream took off on its own, or maybe he was remembering exactly what had happened. The preacher spun him round and round until Boyd rocketed out of his grasp and sailed into the middle of the river, socking down into the cold water, somersaulting, and in the greenish underwater light he'd found himself face-to-face with a long grinning gar. Beneath the surface, the water was clear. In the distance, downriver, he could see people's underpants and their pale naked legs.

That was the dream. Ever since he was five, he'd said grace with his eyes wide open, while he reached out to butter his bread.

Four months along, Sandra sat cross-legged on the floor, drinking herbal tea. She had with her a bag of her old clothes, which she would donate to the hospital, and now she gave directions as he draped them on the mannequin. "Try the blouson top with the straight skirt. I'll never fit into a straight skirt again." She smoothed her denim maternity jumper over her knees. Clumsily Boyd buttoned the clothing on the mannequin. With her blonde wig, she was beautiful.

"I used to love playing with dolls," Sandra said. "Then one day I took my best one and stuck her head under a rocking chair and rocked until her head broke. The stuff that came out looked like cornmeal." She looked troubled. "Why did I do that?"

She finished her tea and went into the bedroom to take a nap. After awhile he went in and lay down beside her.

"Don't you think we should get married?" he said. She seemed like a gentle older sister whose honor he would defend to the death.

Sandra said, "Some things about you bother me. Your eye contact isn't real good. You're younger than I am. Why should we throw in our lots together?"

He reached out and placed his hand on her stomach. "Please, Sandra."

"Oh, all right," she said, and over the next few days, they made their plans and were married.

He sold his house and moved into Sandra's. She lived on a rough little bluff overlooking Lynchburg, but despite the high ground, the mosquitoes at night were ferocious, their hellish whines drilling his ears till he got up, exhausted, and went downstairs to the living room where the air was cooler. Sandra slept deeply, snoring, the moonlight making her gray hair sparkle. When they were dating, he'd never spent much time at her house, even though it was nicer than his and she had a lot of furniture. Now her house felt strange, but in a good way, like visiting a grandmother's house. He wasn't used to the powdery way it smelled.

It was late summer. He discovered that Sandra had planted a corn patch in her backyard, with a few watermelon vines and thorny, fleshy squash. Now the cornstalks stood high and rustly, showing red-brown silk at the tops of the ears. Crows were eager for the corn. Bold and sly, their big black shapes folded deep into the rows of stalks, taking their fill, until Boyd remembered the mannequin.

In Sandra's old prom gown, the mannequin made an elegant scarecrow. Boyd looped the yellow ruffled skirt over one arm and raised her other arm toward the sky. Her smile seemed to deepen, as if she were pleased with her dotted swiss dress and her new job. Once she was installed, with her back to the house and her face to the corn, the crows kept their distance.

"The sun's going to ruin that dress," Boyd told Sandra. "You sure you don't want to wear it anymore?"

"I wore it my junior year, when I went to the prom with the Polish guy who ate grapefruit with the peel on. Senior year I had a prettier dress, a pink one, but he didn't ask me, and nobody else did either."

She looked so hurt at the memory that Boyd patted her hand, trying to think of something gallant to say.

Sandra said, "Seeds were nothing to him. After eating peel, who cares about seeds?"

Sandra wouldn't slow down her schedule or change her early morning shift. She was up and gone before Boyd was awake, leaving him asleep in the warm sheets. While he lay dozing, he would hear the front door open windily, as if pushed by a gale, and then he'd hear the squeaking steps as Sandra's crepe-soled shoes bore her new heavy weight upstairs.

"What did you forget?" he'd call out groggily, sitting up, his heart pounding, for what if it weren't Sandra but some stranger come to kill him?

Always the footsteps died away before they reached the landing. Always, when he asked Sandra about it at supper time, she said, "I didn't come home. I never forget anything. You must've been dreaming."

Maybe he only imagined that things slid around in the house. Water glasses did figure-eights on the dinner table, just little ones that he saw if he watched closely. The shower curtain stuck to him as if hands were pressing through it. Doors popped open, and there were lots of funny sounds, but Sandra said she didn't hear them.

One evening—their six-week anniversary—they sent out for pizza. It didn't come. So much time went by that the lights of Lynchburg winked out slowly on the hill beneath them. They could go out on their front porch and see the lights that marked the ice factory, the dairy, the baseball park, and the bridge. They went upstairs to their bedroom and Boyd rubbed Sandra's back. They fell asleep and woke up so hungry for that pepperoni and cheese and sausage that Boyd finally called the pizza place and was told, "Somebody called back and canceled you-all's order; that's why we didn't deliver it."

"Somebody canceled it?" Boyd said. He hung up, shaken. "There's a dern ghost in this house, Sandra, believe me."

"Oh, they just forgot our order," Sandra said.

There was nothing in the house to eat but hard-boiled eggs. Boyd put some on a plate with a cut-up apple and took it upstairs to her.

"Happy six-week anniversary," they told each other.

A few hours later, Boyd woke to distant thunder, and he thought immediately of the mannequin facing a storm unprotected. He got out of bed, found a big sturdy umbrella, and went outside to the corn patch, where lightning lit the mannequin's figure in brilliant flashbulb pops. Jauntily she stood guard as the rising wind tossed her frilly dress about her body. With twine he lashed the umbrella to her stiff wrist. The cornstalks smelled musty and secretive. Sweet raindrops drummed into his hair. Wind knocked the umbrella from the mannequin's fragile grip so that it swung down defiantly, exposing her to the storm. Silvery snail-trails of rain flowed from her blonde hair down her fine skin.

He worked her feet free from the earth and picked her up, careful not to let the dress drag on the ground. He held the umbrella over both of them. He took her onto the back porch and brushed her off, in case grasshoppers or ants had nested in her gown, and he laid her on the back porch swing, drawing her arms close to her sides. In the blue lightning, she was looking at him with strange sad concentration. He leaned down and kissed her cheek. Wind set the swing to rocking.

Upstairs again, he found Sandra sitting up in bed, her face white. "I dreamed I lost the baby," she said and started to cry.

He put his arms around her. The hard melon of her stomach pressed against his hip.

"You'll be fine," he whispered. He soothed her until she slept. He listened to the porch swing creaking as the storm subsided.

"A little boy came in today," Sandra said one day. "Eight years old. He was orange. He'd drunk too much carrot juice, his mother told me. Imagine letting your kid guzzle so much carrot juice he turns orange."

"Maybe it happened so gradually she didn't notice," Boyd said. "If he drank a lot of grape juice, would that counteract the orange?"

Sandra stared at him. "His mother asked me the

same thing. She got on my nerves. She stubbed her toe going into the emergency room and complained about that the whole time."

"Just how orange was he?"

"Orange enough," said Sandra, threading a needle, squinting as she sewed an appliqué of a duck on a white baby jacket. "He said he wants to stay orange."

"He can probably see real well."

"Do you know these people, Boyd? That's what the child said he was trying to do—improve his vision. It didn't help. He wears thick glasses. He asked me if people can really die of tarantula bites. Got happy when I said yes."

"I hope our kid'll wonder about stuff like that."

"Do you miss being alone, Boyd?" She laid her sewing aside and looked at him, her face bland.

"Aren't you glad we're together, Sandra?" The uncertainty that was always with him hardened into gristle in his heart.

"I've never been like those people over in India, who want to have a whole bunch of children just so somebody'll take care of them when they're old."

"We're only talking about one baby," said Boyd.

"Three months to go," she said. "Three more months to look ugly and feel terrible. Why do you have to be so big and fat? This baby's monster-size."

"You look beautiful, Sandra," he said. He felt a rush of love for her. She looked so vulnerable. Her widow's peak gave her angry face an owlish air, and she had on a smock his mother had given her, with silly pink rick-rack around the neckline and sleeves.

"If I could have one wish right now," she said, "it would be to spank that orange boy's mother. I've been mad at her all day long. I'd spank the orange boy too." She picked up her sewing and stabbed the needle through the duck's eye. "And another thing. Stop tormenting me with that dern doll. I was scared to death when I saw it on the swing this morning."

He opened his mouth to laugh, but she scowled at him. He said, "Do you want me to get rid of it?"

"Oh, let it be a scarecrow. Everybody around here has a job to do." She looked up at him. "That morbid orange boy asked me if I'd ever seen anybody with their head cut off. Had I ever seen a broken bone sticking out of somebody's leg? What do they do with the stuff they pump out of people's stomachs? Just because I'm a nurse, people think I don't get grossed out."

"You can be grossed out whenever you want to be." Boyd leaned down, kissed her cheek, and took the newspaper out on the porch and read it until bedtime. The yellow drum of the September moon gave enough light to see by.

Already his life with Sandra had a steeped quality, familiar and tame. So why did his heart pound so much of the time, and why was his throat dry? Was he worried about the baby?

When he went back inside the house, Sandra was watching an ice skating show on TV. Slim strong figures leaped and twirled, their shiny costumes tighter than skin, their skates as fast as rockets, bearing them across the bluish ice.

"Shouldn't you try to get more rest?" he said.

"You go on up," she said, her eyes on the skaters. "I want to see 'em fall."

The next day, he got off duty early, bought roses from the florist, and drove to the hospital. When he reached Sandra's floor, the head nurse told him she was busy, so he sat down in the waiting room. A stack of notecards on the coffee table caught his eye, and he picked them up.

They were condolence notes, penned in a round backhand, each to a different person. He read them. "Dear Mrs. Jackson, I am sorry to hear of the loss of your husband Lamarr 'Rabbit' Jackson. Though I did not know him, I am sure he was an awesome human being. Yours truly, Darcy Boatwright." "Dear Mr. Sawyer, Your wife's demise has made me sad. I see that she was 93. I know Jesus will be glad to have her. With sympathy forever, Darcy Boatwright." "Dear Surviving Nieces of William 'Cap'n Loopy' Collier, Your grand-uncle's death has made me feel very bad—"

"What are you doing?" someone screamed to Boyd.

Boyd looked up, the notes slipping out of his hands, to see a suntanned child in thick glasses snatching the writing things from the table and stuffing them into a book bag, and realized he was face to face with the orange boy.

"Kindly give me those notecards," the boy said.

Wordlessly, Boyd held them out, and the boy took them and stowed them in the bag. He kept one bandaged forefinger elaborately in the air. "Where's my newspaper?" he demanded.

Boyd discovered that he was sitting on it. It was the local paper, folded to the obituary section, with names checked off. The boy stuffed this in the bag too. "And I have black-bordered envelopes," he said. "Where are they?" He searched energetically under the table and between the vinyl sofa cushions.

"—some more tests made," came Sandra's voice from the corridor, and then Sandra appeared, her hands full of clipboards, accompanied by a woman somehow familiar to Boyd.

"The same thing happened with sour cream," the woman said to Sandra. "He ate a ton of it until finally he got allergic to it."

The boy straightened up, holding the bandaged forefinger commandingly in front of him. "I am not allergic to carrot juice. I just vomited one time."

The boy's mother craned her neck back and forth as if working a crick out of it. Her hair was very short and she had thin hoops in her ears.

"—to rule anything out," Sandra told the woman. Sandra saw Boyd and said, "This is my husband. Boyd, this is Delilah Boatwright and her son Darcy."

"Mother, let's go," said Darcy, sounding offended.

"Do you have your letters?" Delilah asked him.

"I can't find my envelopes," Darcy said.

Boyd saw a corner of a small, black-bordered stationery box beneath a stack of magazines, but a perverse impulse kept him from saying anything.

"I had them already addressed," the orange boy said. "I always do that first."

"Well, regular envelopes will have to do," the boy's mother said, frowning vaguely at Boyd. "You bought a blonde one," she said.

"Remember, Delilah—Sunday," Sandra said.

"Sunday," said the orange boy's mother. "See ya." She led her son away.

"The wig woman," said Boyd, watching them go.

"I've had a change of heart about Delilah," Sandra said. "I feel for her. She's raising Darcy all by herself, and she said the demand for wigs in Lynchburg isn't what it should be. Plus, she's a safety patrol at her son's school. I invited them over for a cookout."

"We don't have a grill," Boyd said.

"So buy one."

He handed her the flowers. Already the heavy yellow blossoms were blackish at the rims. "Sandra, can you leave early? We could go somewhere nice for supper."

"Boyd, you're so good to me," she said, sounding annoyed. "There they are," and she bent down and plucked the box of envelopes from their hiding place.

"Sandra, there's something wrong with that kid. More than just carrot juice."

"I think his sympathy cards are sweet. Delilah said he saves his allowance to buy the stationery." She looked at her watch. "I guess I can leave."

As he maneuvered the pickup truck out of the hospital parking lot and onto the main road, he drove carefully, not wanting to jar Sandra. It was a lazy lavender afternoon, and they drove with their windows down, not talking. From the ditches, thickets of kudzu gave off a tangy gasoline scent. They went to a place they had favored when they were dating and got barbecue, coleslaw, and hush puppies with honey. A country and western band played, but Boyd and Sandra just sat and watched the dancers.

He reflected on how they had met. He'd fallen off his roof and broken his arm, and there in the hospital was Sandra, gentle as she helped the doctor. Unlike the other nurses, she hadn't made small talk. He'd found himself trying to draw her out. He wondered what it would be like to be married to a talkative woman.

"Ready to go?" Boyd said. Sandra stood up. Her weight made her awkward now. Back in the truck, Boyd steered toward home, but as they passed the field beside the newspaper office, they saw carnival booths and a little carousel, its lights purple and red in the dusk, and Sandra said, "Let's stop!" He parked beside the field and they got out.

They bought cotton candy. Its sugary, spidery stickiness caught in Boyd's beard. They stood abstractedly as people swirled around them. Cap guns made sharp pops in the shooting booths, and calliope music pumped and piped. It was too early for a big crowd. Teenagers gathered in self-conscious groups, and children chased each other, spilling their snowcones.

"Look, a professional age-guesser," Sandra said. She strode to a booth where a man leaned idly on the counter, surrounded by stuffed animals hanging from hooks.

"Guess me," she told the man.

"Two dollars. I keep it if I'm within five years," he said, and Boyd paid. The man shut his eyes and made Sandra write her age on a piece of paper.

Then the man opened his eyes and stared at Sandra. Boyd didn't like his mean gaze, his hard, bald head, his dirty overalls, or the cracked lips that he licked and pursed. The man looked at Sandra's neck. He made her turn around. Sandra held herself proudly, shaking back her ponytail. At last the man said, "Fifty."

Sandra's face froze. She showed the man the paper on which she had written thirty-nine.

"Pick out a critter," said the man carelessly. He lit a cigar and jerked his chin toward the stuffed animals suspended like hams from the ceiling of his booth.

Boyd touched Sandra's arm. "Let's go."

"I'm supposed to get an animal, and I'm going to," she said harshly. She reached up and pulled a stuffed monkey from a hook. It had yellow eyes, stiff arms, and loose legs. It wore a blue diaper and a Mexican hat with sequins.

"That's the best of 'em," the man said, blowing smoke.

Sandra clutched it to her chest. She said, "Do you know a man named Les Waleski? He used to work at carnivals."

"Never heard of him." The man turned away from her.

Boyd and Sandra walked back to the car. "I just thought, well, it wouldn't hurt to ask. That's who I went to the prom with," Sandra said. Her voice had a hitch in it.

"I'd like to knock that guy over," said Boyd. "Cheap circus carney."

She dropped the monkey and gripped her stomach.

"Sandra!" he cried, and reached out to steady her, but she held him off, breathing deeply.

"That barbecue didn't agree with me," she said. She picked up the monkey and climbed into the truck. "You know what Darcy Boatwright does? He eats Alka-Seltzer tablets without any water, like they're Swee-Tarts. Maybe I'll try that." She jounced the monkey on her knee. "Maybe that guy *was* Les Waleski, and for some reason, he didn't want me to recognize him."

"Want me to drive you back so you can tell him to go to hell?" Boyd said.

"I only tell people to go to hell when I'm alone with them," she said.

The orange boy could yodel, and on Sunday, full of grilled steak, macaroni salad, sliced tomatoes, fried egg-plant, and coconut cream pie, he proved it, so loudly that Boyd's ears rang, and he told Darcy, "That's enough." Darcy's mother frowned at Boyd.

So did Sandra. "I like yodeling," she said.

They were sitting on the back porch. It was a hot, bright noon. The mannequin stood guard over the corn patch, but the crows were less afraid of her now, and they wheeled around in big bobbly circles, as if hoping she would welcome them in for a feast. The prom gown was bleached almost white. Delilah looked at the mannequin as if she were an old acquaintance she couldn't quite place.

"A man proposed to me last night," Delilah said, examining her fingernails. "I met him at a fried chicken place, and twenty minutes later he asked me to marry him. He has two farms. He owns one himself and he runs the other one for some people who live somewhere else. His wife left him. The poor fellow's desperate just to *talk* to a woman."

"What did you tell him?" asked Sandra. She leaned forward admiringly, pushing the salad bowl away with her elbow.

"I felt too sorry for him to give him a direct no, but I sure didn't say yes," said Delilah. "My safety patrol instincts came into play. Stop, look, listen." She smiled at Boyd, and he was reminded, as he'd been in the wig store, of a cat yawning.

"Guess what. Boyd thinks my—our—house is haunted," Sandra said. "He hears footsteps coming up the stairs after I leave for work in the morning."

"Neato," said Darcy. He narrowed his eyes at Boyd.

Boyd didn't want Sandra to go on. The matter of the ghost was somehow private. "It's just wind," he said.

"Have you felt any cold spots?" Delilah asked Boyd. "What's a big guy like you afraid of a ghost for?"

Boyd glared at her. She lifted her root beer and took a pull from it, eyeing him.

"I'd say fee, fie, fo, fum," Darcy declared. "Did anybody die here in a bad way? Have you thought about that, Sandra? Or is it the spirit of your baby, being a poltergeist?"

Sandra looked unnerved. "I hadn't thought about that."

Suddenly Boyd was certain that the baby would be born dead. He said, "Darcy, don't you ever write us one of those sympathy cards. No matter what."

"What on earth is wrong with you?" asked Delilah, staring at him. "Darcy's sensitive. He had a nervous breakdown when he was five. He'd built a snowman, and a neighbor kid came over and ate the head off it. Darcy freaked. Anyway, getting back to the guy with two farms."

"Is he cute?" asked Sandra.

"I'd say he used to be, and could be again, but he's not real cute right now. I wish he would just give me one of those farms."

Boyd decided that when Delilah and Darcy were gone, he'd tell Sandra he didn't want them to come over anymore. He pictured himself in a booth at a restaurant, proposing marriage to this confident cat-faced woman with her silver earrings.

Delilah said, "You know what that farmer said to me?

'I've hardly ever been out of the county, but if you'd go with me, I'd take you to more wonderful places on this earth than you've ever known to be.'" To Darcy, Delilah said, "Finish up, we've got to be going."

Sandra made them wait while she wrapped up a plate of leftover steak and macaroni salad. "I usually put grated carrots in the salad, but not today," she said, handing the plate to Darcy.

"Don't even say it," Darcy said. "I can get through the day if I don't hear the word."

When they were gone, Boyd asked Sandra, "When was the last time the baby moved? It's been a long time since you talked about feeling it move."

"The baby's all right," she said. Angrily she stared at the mannequin. "Get rid of that mannequin, Boyd. I'll never be young and thin again. Maybe I'll want the baby once it's born. Now leave me alone." She burst into tears and stepped into the house, leaving him with the plates of food on the table. A wasp settled on a golden slice of tomato.

He walked the few short steps from the porch to where the mannequin kept vigil. He almost tapped her on the shoulder, so real did she seem as she stood there with the breeze in her beautiful hair. He carried her to the garage and stood her against a worktable, amid the dusty, dusky shapes of lawn mower and wheelbarrow. Flyspecked windows cast grainy shadows across the mannequin's high cheeks. He took a long time arranging a space for her, making sure no oil or sawdust could spatter her gown.

"You don't have a ghost in your house," he imagined her saying. "That's all wind. But you *do* love another woman, sure as the crows will eat the corn. What can you do, once a child has started, and once you're man and wife?"

The next morning, he couldn't help himself. He drove by the elementary school, where the safety patrols were on duty—three or four women wearing bright yellow slickers in the warm rain, directing groups of children to cross the street or pause on the corner. There in the intersection was Delilah, her hair tucked beneath a visored cap, her stance theatrical as she held out both arms to the children: *Come to me.* School buses turned when she told them to. She didn't use an umbrella. She held her head high.

He pulled up to the intersection, hoping she wouldn't notice him. She was facing him, her makeup perfect despite the rain, her eyes dramatically lined, her arms outspread: *Come to me.*

He edged his pickup truck around her. She looked through his windshield and waved to him, but he ignored the wave and the catlike smile that seemed to leap through the wet glass at him.

Shaken, he sped down the street. He had the day off, and he spent it buying baby things, determined to get everything on the list Sandra had given him. He found shoes and blankets at a department store.

For the antique cradle and high chair, he drove out of town, past the dump, and stopped at a ramshackle secondhand store. It was just a shed crammed with household goods and old books. Rain fell harder, with a sound like tapping fingers on the shed's makeshift plastic roof. He found an oak high chair and cradle, carved with serious setting-sun faces, side by side in a corner, as if they'd been put there just for him. He hauled them out and tested the cradle; it rocked slow and gentle.

He remembered his mother saying that if you didn't turn a child in its cradle, its head would go flat in the back and it would grow up that way, with a funny thin wedge of a head. He'd turn his child over. His child would have a perfect head.

Come to me.

He lugged the chair and cradle to the front of the shed, where the clerk, a tiny old woman, named a price. She wrapped a cobweb around her thin fingers.

He put the things into his truck and headed back to town. He remembered how his parents had played with him when he was a baby, gently tossing him back and forth between them, their arms held out the way Delilah's had been. They'd never known how terrified and thrilled he was, to be flying one instant and falling the next.

White Lilies

WHEN DREW Schultz was fifteen, he went to a blue-grass concert near Warrenton, out by Lake Whippoor-will. The lake was really just a big pond, flat as a silver dish and studded around the edges with Dutch iris. Drew could hear the music from way off, even before he got there. He was with his guitar teacher, Mr. Hixon, and Mr. Hixon's wife. Drew had always called him "Mr. Hixon," but today, as they drove over from Manassas in Mr. Hixon's red Pinto with the Statler Brothers on the radio, Mr. Hixon said to call him "Nate," and he intro-duced his wife as "Lemon." In the hour since then, Drew had twice got up the courage to call Mr. Hixon "Nate," but he could only call Lemon "you."

So here they were at the biggest bluegrass festival ever held in Virginia, and the whole world was here with them—grannies in rocking chairs, little kids in cowboy hats, long-haired men and women in tiny wire-rimmed glasses, the men's hands delicate, the women's hands like men's, and up on a big wooden platform, semicircular around the lake, were the musicians. Mr. Hixon said that Johnny Cash's mother-in-law was there, and Drew laughed. It struck him as funny that somebody like Johnny Cash would have a mother-in-law.

Nate Hixon said, in a hushed voice, "Look, that's Earl Scruggs!"

"Where?" Drew craned his neck.

"Waving his guitar." Mr. Hixon pronounced it *git*-tar. So that was how you said it at a bluegrass festival.

They sat on a scratchy red plaid afghan that Lemon spread on the ground, but because of the crowd it was hard to see anything if you were sitting down, so Drew kept standing up and looking around. He felt he'd been moving toward this day all his life. Lemon sat cross-legged, drinking from a thermos. Suddenly she reached up and tugged on the fringed shawl of a woman standing close by and said, "Maureen!"

The woman whirled around: "Lemon!" and sank down beside Drew. The fringe of her shawl brushed his arm. The two women embraced. Drew smelled Maureen's perfume: cinnamon?

"How *are* you?" Lemon asked, blowing cigarette smoke out of the corner of her mouth.

"Looking for a place to live, as usual," came the answer. "I talk to myself, and it tends to unnerve roommates. God knows what I actually *say*. I have people in my head all the time, and I do talk with them, or imitate them, in barks and whispers, that kind of thing. And who is this?" She turned to Drew, and he found himself staring at her eyebrows, which were sharply peaked like the hands of a clock saying 8:20. It was the first time he'd ever really thought about somebody's eyebrows. Beneath them, the woman's eyes were blue pinwheels. Her skin was so freckled that it gave the impression of being many different colors.

Lemon said, "Drew Schultz, Maureen Mallory. He's one of Nate's students, Maureen."

"Can you play *On Top of Old Smokey?*" Maureen asked him. "That's the first piece Nate taught me to play. Never got much beyond it."

"I can play that and some other stuff too."

"My boyfriend is supposed to meet me here," Maureen said, turning to Lemon, "but how will he ever find me? What does it mean when you arrange to meet someone in a crowd of thousands? That you don't care if he finds you or not?"

Drew hunched closer, enthralled. He watched as Maureen lifted something from her big, shapeless pocketbook: a packet of little white wrappers and a sack of pot. As she rolled herself a joint, she said, "Drew, don't ever become a psychotherapist. You'll find that all your patients are just spoiled brats whose families are sick of giving them sympathy, but still give them money to dump on a hired ear." She offered him the joint. It was stronger than anything he'd smoked before, and soon he felt better than ever.

He and Maureen lay back on the afghan while the Hixons danced nearby, sometimes stumbling onto

Drew and Maureen and then smiling, "Sorry, you two." Maureen told Drew that her boyfriend was actually one of her patients. He was spoiled beyond belief, and she really didn't like him much, she said.

"Gosh," said Drew.

"You didn't know?" Maureen laughed, showing lovely teeth. "Adults can be spoiled too." She sat up. "I want a hot dog, could you get me one? I saw a guy selling them over there who looks like he just escaped from jail, and they're probably soybean dogs anyway, but what the hey." She dug in her purse for money, but Drew said proudly, "I'll buy it for you."

In a trance, he moved toward the hot dog booth, which was squeezed in between all the people on the other side of the lake. He was noticing everything: people's eyes, the bow in a little girl's hair, a tattoo on a man's arm that said Hooray. I'm happy, he thought. He breathed deeply. The air smelled like what it was: the scent of several thousand humans. For the first time all spring he could forget, briefly, that his father was dying of leukemia.

It took him ages to reach the hot dog booth, and then he had to wait in a long line. When it was finally his turn, the man said, "Sorry, son, ain't no more. I done sold the last 'un."

"Anywhere else I can get one?" He hated the way his voice scaled upward.

"Shoulda brung your lunch, I guess." The man snapped down the aluminum shutter of the booth and Drew turned and looked for his group. The music was very loud now, and the twangy beat rubberized his kneecaps and made him smack the heel of his hand against his thigh. It was chilly for May. He buttoned his baseball jacket. It took him almost ten minutes to get back through the crowd.

There was Lemon, arms akimbo, glaring. He felt a start of fear: was she mad that he'd gone away for a little while? What had he done wrong? He'd been a little afraid of her ever since they were introduced that morning. She resembled a lemon, in a way, with her short round body and pointed blonde head.

But she wasn't looking at him. She was staring at the lumpy form of the plaid afghan, which jerked and rolled on the ground. She kicked it, then grabbed one corner and pulled it away, revealing Nate Hixon and Maureen Mallory lying propped on their elbows, laughing. Maureen tossed a strand of straight black hair out of her face; Nate rolled his eyes.

"Lemon, have a heart," he said.

"We were only kissing," said Maureen.

Lemon said, "It's time to go. Drew, you carry the afghan and thermos to the car. We'll meet you there."

"I want to stay longer!" Drew cried, horrified that he sounded like a child pleading with its mother.

"No," said Lemon. "No, *no.*"

A week later, when he went for his guitar lesson, there was Maureen in the kitchen with Lemon, drinking coffee. He didn't know which one he was more surprised to see. In the six months he'd been taking lessons, he'd never seen Lemon at her own house, had never met her until the day of the festival. Mr. Hixon had said she worked every Saturday at a bakery. Now what?

Maureen swiveled around on her barstool, a mug steaming in her hands. "Hi, stranger. Which should it be, the red or the blue?" She held fabric samples toward him.

He shifted the guitar case on his shoulder.

"For curtains," said Maureen, and she and Lemon giggled.

"Maureen's moving in upstairs," Lemon explained. "We're decorating, Drew. You have to do these things right."

He feigned nonchalance. "The red's okay." It was a gingham print with little birds in white squares.

"What about the bakery?" he asked Lemon, his courage failing him as soon as her eyes met his.

"I quit the bakery, okay? Maybe I just want to stay home and be entertained by my husband's wonderful students."

"Oh."

"Drew, come on back." Mr. Hixon summoned him into the den. Something white and furry scurried away as he entered, and he jumped.

"That's just Maureen's ferret," said Mr. Hixon. "Now let's see what you remember from last week."

Usually, the plain brown den, with its knotty pine paneling and orange-crate coffee table, was the perfect place to learn, but not today. Drew tried to concentrate, but every time he plucked the guitar strings, he imagined the women in the kitchen mocking and deriding him: "No talent at all, dumb kid, mouth hanging open and zits on his face and all he can think about is his dick!"

"Drew, get with it. Last time you did great with this exercise."

His fingers felt as thick and square as the fish sticks his mother often served. Mr. Hixon's voice seemed far away, like water trickling through a radiator pipe. The whole hour, his lesson went badly, and Mr. Hixon shook his head. Drew was ashamed. In his mind, ever since the concert, he'd been playing "Way Downtown," just like the famous musicians at Lake Whippoorwill. Yet here he was, bungling the simplest things. It wasn't a *git*-tar in his hands, just a guitar.

He fumbled through the last exercise and was startled to hear applause behind him: Lemon and Maureen had come into the room. He felt a rush of gladness. It was exciting to be part of this grown-up world, exciting and kind of scary. Mr. Hixon was a renegade at school, wearing his hair long and his sideburns full, and it was natural that he'd be married to somebody like Lemon and have a friend like Maureen.

He reached down to gather his guitar things, and suddenly the room was dark—dark, and he was fighting something, a heavy blanket over him.

"Hey!" he yelped.

The women were laughing. He felt their hands on his shoulders, through the cloth. Yet his impulse was to fight. He could hardly breathe. The wool rubbed his skin. He was bigger than they were, but they held him tight until he was still.

Mr. Hixon said, "What the hell are y'all doing to him?"

"Come with us, Drew," Maureen said, and blindly he followed as she led him—where? Back to the kitchen: he smelled coffee. They made him climb up on a stool and rest his elbows on the counter.

He said, "This better be good." His palms were slick.

"Easy now," said Lemon. They raised the blanket so that his body was free, but kept it over his eyes and the top of his head. "Do it, Maureen," Lemon said.

He felt an icy pressure on one ear. The cold numbed his skin, and then there was a sharp sting.

"Ow!"

"Hold still, hon," said Maureen. "Okay, Lemon, take off the blindfold."

He blinked. His face, in the mirror Maureen held up to him, was somebody else's. There was a tiny gold ring in his right ear. He touched it.

"Now you're cool," said Lemon. She swept the ice pack into the sink and brandished the needle in front of him.

"I like it," he said.

Maureen leaned over and kissed him on the mouth. Mr. Hixon put Tommy James and the Shondells on the stereo as loud as it would go, and Lemon got out the pot and the wrappers and started rolling.

"Crystal Blue Persuasion," Drew grinned. "Love it."

Several hours later, Nate Hixon flipped him the keys to the Pinto. "Go to McDonald's, Drew, and bring us some burgers."

He only had his learner's permit. Driving by himself, he was scared. But he got there and got the food and brought it back, and then he felt proud.

As they ate, they smoked regular cigarettes. Cavalierly he answered the questions they put to him. Did he have a girlfriend, Lemon wanted to know. Yeah, he said, secretly reckoning that he'd had enough conversations with girls and had been present at enough mixed gatherings to constitute having a girlfriend. And, of course, there was that swift episode in the poolhouse last summer, with the girl that all the other guys had done it with, though he'd been so nervous and it had happened so fast that he hadn't enjoyed it much.

"So you *do* have a girlfriend?" Maureen pressed. "You're getting all red. We don't want to embarrass you, honey. It's just that our lives are so boring."

"I bet you're a virgin," said Lemon. Her eyes challenged him. She raised her arms and twisted her long thin hair into a knot on her head. Her nipples stuck out against her black T-shirt.

The others waited, leaning toward him over the kitchen table. He picked up his hamburger and chewed it deliberately, while his mind groped. Should he pull a stunt, like go to the phone and pretend to call a girl and say all sorts of dirty stuff into the receiver? Should he lean over and french-kiss Lemon? He was keyed in to what they liked.

"You're very rude, Lemon," he said at last, so calmly that it fit. It floored them.

"Mr. Cool!" said Maureen. "Give me some of your fries." He held one in front of her face. When she reached up to take it, he caught her hand and brought the french fry to her lips. She touched it with her tongue, her eyes on his.

Mr. Hixon laughed. "Good grief. Look, Drew, want to go skeet shooting with us?"

He wanted to go but he was afraid that any minute they would tire of him and drop him.

Mr. Hixon put on an exaggerated Southern accent. He reached out and squeezed the back of Lemon's neck. "My wife here's from an ole Virginia fam'ly and they do things like skeet shootin' on a Sa'rday afternoon."

Lemon stood up and gathered the trash from their meal. Drew finished his Coke. "That's okay," he said. "I gotta go."

"Is that a yes or a no?" asked Lemon. She slam-dunked a ball of paper napkins into the trash can.

"I'm not going either," Maureen said. "I'm tired."

"Women are always tired," said Mr. Hixon. "Let's go," he commanded Lemon. She put on a cowboy hat and a suede jacket.

"Bye," said Mr. Hixon, waving his arm to Maureen

and Drew. Lemon said nothing as she went out the door.

"Bye," said Drew and Maureen. When the Hixons were gone, Drew and Maureen looked at each other and laughed. Drew felt lighthearted and carefree. He realized that with a woman, you just had to have laughter.

He was ready. He took Maureen's hand. "What does the upstairs of this place look like?" he asked her. "Where're you gonna hang those curtains?"

"Tell me a secret about yourself," said Maureen. They lay warmly beneath her pink and brown quilt in the guest room. Unpacked boxes made shadowy shapes around the bed and gave off a cardboardy smell. He wanted to check his watch, but he felt too numb and lazy to reach for it on the nightstand.

"A secret? You know some of 'em now." He laughed and tumbled her over on her back, but her face stopped him.

"I mean a real secret."

"Okay." He took a deep breath, thinking. "I remember everything that happens to me."

"So do I. In times of stress, things sear in."

"But I mean *everything*. It doesn't matter how much happens or how much time goes by. Nothing ever gets—" he used a word he'd never spoken before— "vague. Like the bluegrass concert—I remember exactly what the people looked like who were sitting next to us, and what the hot dog guy said to me, and I'll remember those things for a long time. I can remember exactly

where everybody sat in my second-grade class. I just
don't forget."

"Then why can't you play the guitar better?"

"I don't know."

"And do you get all A's? Schoolwork's mostly memory, isn't it?"

"I don't get many A's." He moved away from her a
little. She seemed suddenly like a teacher. "What's your
secret?"

She laughed. "I know how I'm going to die."

"How? Are you sick?"

"No. But I know how my life will end."

"You can't know that," said Drew.

"It happens over and over in a dream. I'm riding in
the back of a truck, and there's a dog with me, like I've
just gone somewhere, with somebody, to help them
pick out a hunting dog. I don't know who's driving. It's
dark and it's fall, and the air smells great, and then it's
like I can see this happen from way up above the road:
the truck drives under this overpass, which is real low,
so low that because I'm tall and I'm standing up, my
head smashes right into it, and I die. Blood shoots out
like berries."

"Then don't ever ride in the back of a truck! Don't
ever get in a truck with a dog!" He sat up, curling a pil-
low into his stomach, his hands on her shoulders. She
raised her pointed eyebrows at him.

"It's my insurance. If things ever get too bad, I'll set it
up and everybody'll think it's an accident." She got out
of bed, went to the window, lit a cigarette, and blew

smoke through the screen. She was naked; her white skin glowed in the late sunshine.

"It's just a dream," Drew said.

"And dreams are my science."

He thought of the roads around Manassas, the old ones in the woods near the battlefield, with their bridges and cutoffs, and wondered if she had one in mind. "My dad says heaven's like the battlefield park. He works there as a guide."

Her pursed lips, blowing smoke, whistled like a train. "That's sweet."

"My dad's real sick, Maureen." He never talked about it with anybody, but he wanted to talk about it with her. He opened his mouth to go on, but she interrupted.

"Sick? I'll tell you about sick. My husband was sick in the head." Her face went ugly, her upper lip curling out of shape. She came back to the bed and lay down stiffly, as if her muscles hurt. "He used to beat me up. He was crazy. He set a church on fire and then a school. I moved across three states to get away from him!"

He was almost angry at her. He felt she had ignored the news of his father's illness. She hadn't seemed to take it in at all. But her face was so troubled that he prompted, "What happened to him?"

"He's dead. I didn't hear from him for a long time, and then the police called me and said they'd found a body underneath a tree with a rope on it. It was him. He'd hanged himself and hung there so long he'd started to rot." She sucked on the cigarette so hard he thought she would eat it.

The overpass story had made him respond, but that was a dream and this was real. He didn't know what to say. He reached out and stroked her hair; there were a few grays in it. She was old: twenty-seven?

They heard the front door open. The Hixons were home.

"Oh, no!" Drew said, leaping out of bed and scrambling for his jeans. Maureen laughed, relaxing again, pushing the quilt back with long white legs.

"They don't care," she said.

"Lemon doesn't like me," said Drew.

Maureen stood up and shimmied into a shiny blue slip. "They're not part of this anymore. Now it's just us."

At supper, his father pointed to the earring. "What's this?"

"All the guys are gettin' 'em," Drew mumbled.

"Did it hurt?"

"No."

"I got somethin' new today, too," said his father. He pulled himself around in his chair and held up his legs, encased in high, shiny leather boots. Drew stared. His father never bought anything that expensive.

"Aren't they nice?" his mother said. "They look just like cavalry boots."

"They'll last me on my march into the next world," said his father.

His mother laid her fork down and pressed her fingertips to her temples. She said, "Don't you think it could just be cat scratch fever? Doctors can be wrong. Please don't sound so *ready*."

"They wouldn't be wrong this long," his father said. "It's not any cat fever. It's leukemia."

"I talked with the preacher again today," his mother said. "He told me God's testing me for some reason."

"All preachers say that, no matter what the problem is," his father said. "It's supposed to make you feel mysterious and important all at once, and the preacher gets the credit. I hate preachers. Their view of life is so dern dark."

"Well, I can *try* to feel better, can't I?" said his mother. She pushed her plate away. "Don't give me any more of that crap about everybody's got to go, or your number coming up. It's bad enough knowing I'll never be happy again."

Drew rearranged the meat loaf on his plate. "What did we used to talk about?" he asked. "Just this afternoon I told somebody I could remember everything, but I can't."

They stared at him. His father said, "Like before I got sick?"

"Yeah. Like what did we used to talk about?"

"Come on, let's go for a walk," his father said.

On the battlefield—where during the day his father was a park ranger—a few tourists pitted their cameras against the ebbing daylight. Drew and his father scoped around the edge of the woods and went down to Bull Run. The little bridge arched above them. They could hear a few children shouting behind the trees and the traffic whispering far off on Route 66, but other than that it was quiet. The creek made a steady meditating sound like thinking out loud. A bullfrog sprang into it.

Drew said, "Whenever I'm out here, I can almost forget there's school and the mall and movies and TV."

His father caught him by the shoulders so they stood face to face. His features looked small and angry and pushed together. "What about pot? Do you forget about that too?" He hit Drew hard across the face. "I smelled it on your clothes. Damn it, Drew, I'da thought you'd be smart enough not to fool with that stuff. And here you go smokin' pot and puttin' a earring in your ear. Where's your guitar, anyway?"

"My guitar?"

"You didn't bring it home with you from your lesson. Did you go to that guitar lesson or what?"

"Yeah, I went. I must've left it at the Hixons'." He'd forgotten the guitar completely. His cheek hurt, yet he didn't resent the slap. For so many months his father had been jolly and even-tempered about dying, it was a relief to see him mad again.

"I've smoked lots of pot," Drew said. "You just never caught me before."

For an instant there was combat in his father's brown eyes but then the affability came back. "You've got to be reliable, Drew. By nature, I ain't the reliable type, but I learned how to be."

"I don't know what to say to Mom when she's upset."

"And you won't know what to say to her when I'm dead, either. All we can do is be brave."

They climbed up the short bank to the bridge, their feet stirring the thick red dust. "Brave, this was brave," his father said. "Practical, at least: the Yanks at Cold Harbor. That morning in July, they knew it'd be big, knew we'd beat 'em bad. So they pinned pieces of paper to their uniforms with their names and addresses on 'em."

Drew had grown up with the Civil War: he remembered the centennial reenactment of the battle of Manassas, when his father had donned a gray uniform and borrowed a big chestnut gelding and ridden off to war. Drew was about six. He and his mother worked their way through the crowd of spectators to see the clashing lines of soldiers. The men were firing blanks, but still the fumes were harsh and acrid and Drew tasted the smoke on his tongue. His ears drummed from the yells and cannonfire. The horses, their forelegs cycling in the air, certainly believed it was real war. His mother had kept pointing to the melee and saying, "There's your father. No, I guess not." Drew had been surprised, that day in 1961, that the grass was green, the sky blue, instead of the foreboding half-tones of the old photographs, where even summer landscapes looked always pocked with fine snow.

Now he said, "I don't want to talk about people getting blown up and shot."

His father brushed this off. "You don't just learn stories, you inherit 'em. When I'm in a battle reenactment, I know things I got no way on earth of knowing, and all I can figure is they're memories in my genes. I was born old. It's been a fine life." He took a jew's harp from his pocket and held it to his lips, twanging out a tune. When he was finished he jabbed the heel of his boot into the dust on the bridge. "I hope my patch of heaven is half this pretty."

Drew blurted, "I met a woman who knows how she's going to die. Her head's gonna smash against an overpass."

He was horrified that he had revealed this. His tongue was a trip wire.

His father looked tired, but he laughed. "She was just trying to impress you. Girls do that same as guys."

As they headed home, Drew's thoughts stayed on Maureen. The thing was, he believed her. She did know how she was going to die. And that story about her husband: that was her history, her battle.

Her cinnamon cologne came back to him, her skin and her touch. It wasn't her fault about her husband or her death dream, he told himself. But he couldn't stand it. A rope, she'd said, a rope with a body on it.

He heard the children playing in the woods behind the battlefield, their cries growing fainter, and he longed to join them. He didn't want to take lessons with Nate Hixon anymore. He dreaded going back for his guitar.

It was dusk when they got home. His mother was in the kitchen eating the supper that she had been too upset to eat earlier.

"The preacher came by," she said. "He brought all the Easter lilies that were left over from last month. We put them on the back porch. They're so pretty. Wasn't that nice of him?"

Drew and his parents went to the back porch and his mother opened the door and waved a hand over the lilies. There were a dozen, tall, creamy, and wilted in their pink foil-covered pots. They gave off a powerful scent. Grouped together on the porch, they made a presence: instinctively Drew recoiled. Behind him, his father stiffened.

"Funeral flowers," his father whispered.

"No, honey, just flowers," said his mother.

"I ain't dead yet!" his father said. His face contorted. "I know that's how it'll *be,* but I ain't dead yet."

"They're nothing, they're just flowers," his mother wept.

"Get 'em out of here," his father said. His mother bent awkwardly to obey, but the pots were too heavy and they resisted when she tried to lift them.

"I'll do it," Drew said. Behind him he heard his father sob. His father's boots hit the floor hard as he plunged out of the room and up the stairs.

Drew turned back to the plants. His mother touched his shoulder, her wet eyes wavering over him. "Here, Drew, Mr. Hixon brought this by for you."

His guitar. He took it from her. She hurried after his father, her crying muffled as she climbed the stairs. After awhile, the house was quiet.

He put the guitar on the top shelf in the living room closet and closed the door.

The Egg Man

W<small>ILL</small> C<small>LATTERBUCK</small> helped his wife pull the twisted sheets out of the washing machine and pile them into a wicker basket. Together, they carried the basket outside and hung the sheets on the line.

"Morning sun's the bleachingest," Dulcie said around the clothespins in her mouth.

The sun wouldn't be up for an hour, and by then they'd be long on the road—he in his van delivering eggs all over Coahoma County, she driving a yellow school bus. In the cool pre-dawn, the only light came from the damp pale sheets themselves.

Will plucked something else from the laundry pile, a ruffled white garment. "What's this?"

Dulcie snatched it and shook it out. "Bloomers, part of my old bathing suit. You used to tell me how sexy I looked in these."

He recalled the Dulcie of twenty years ago—a pretty

girl hogging the covers, stealing the blankets off him in her sleep. She was still appealing, and she kept the house neat and clean.

Dulcie said, "As soon as school's out, I want to go down to Gulf Shores, lie on the beach all day, and get a tan."

"School won't be out for a long time," Will said. It was February: a recent ice storm, freaky and severe, had wrecked trees and power lines from Clarksdale all the way to Memphis, closing the schools for a week.

"Just planning ahead," Dulcie said. They hung the rest of the laundry—overalls, socks, towels, long johns. The bloomers caught the air and billowed fatly.

"Drive safely," Will said and kissed her. She smelled of the deviled ham she had used in their scrambled eggs, and her cheek felt hot.

"Lena Wickham's trying to do a number on me," Dulcie said. Lena Wickham was another bus driver. "She tries to look into my head and put an accident on my route."

"Don't you let her." Will laughed but it came out a yawn. Dulcie dramatized everything—potholes in the road, her astigmatism; he was used to it. He was eager to get to his van, loaded already with fresh eggs that he'd gathered from his generous hens and stacked in cardboard cartons.

"Lena would be glad if I died," Dulcie said. "She'd gloat. It makes me so mad."

"Nobody wants you dead, Dulcie."

The wind pushed the sheets against her, and she held

them off. "It could happen," she said. "That's why I'm so careful. My only luxury, morning and afternoon, is my backscratcher."

Will had seen it often—the slim scratcher with a tiny wooden hand, which Dulcie kept beside her while she drove her bus.

Dulcie picked up the empty basket. "I'll be home before you are," she said and went into the house.

There was a new stop on his route, a place called Heartfield where a religious group lived.

"We need ten dozen eggs a week," a woman had said on the telephone. "Consider it a standing order. Send us a monthly bill."

Winding past a green stretch of winter wheat, Will saw the place, a kind of campus consisting of an old manor house and several new brick cottages.

Proud of referrals, he had asked the woman on the phone, "How did you hear about me?"

"Grapevine," the woman said. "The back door will be unlocked. Just leave the eggs in the kitchen."

He parked in a lot near several late-model, expensive-looking cars. Lifting the egg cartons from the van, he balanced them against his chest and made his way to the back door of the big house, his feet crunching on new gravel.

It was noon. All morning, he had visited homes in the flat Delta countryside, rich and poor, lifting the latches and pushing open the doors, calling hello into the warm silence of an empty house: such was the trust that an egg man gave and got, swiftly pocketing the money left out for him, setting the eggs in humming refrigerators (he and everybody he knew called them iceboxes). His customers knew he would not steal—not a fresh chocolate cake on the kitchen counter, nor a cold six-pack, nor a treasured ring on the windowsill above the sink. Sometimes he was tempted; who wouldn't be, given all the opportunities of being loose in somebody else's house? Tempted by cherry muffins, a pretty flower arrangement, a cute salt-and-pepper set that Dulcie would like. By the very books on people's bookshelves, the bulbs in their lamps, and the lady of the house, who might offer him coffee and a sleepy, dimply smile. Usually, though, he didn't see anybody, as if his route were preordained to be carried out in solitude. The most he might do in those kitchens was drink a glass of water, wash out the glass, and put it back in the cupboard. He might swat a wasp, throw out a dead mouse and rebait the trap with cheese, or stroke the carved cherubs of an old oak sideboard that caught his fancy. Each house had its own smell, of children, soot, gun oil, cologne. He swore he could tell if somebody in the house had been sick that week or had heard some good news.

He had done this for a long time, and before that his father had done it and his grandfather. Their hen dynasty had fed generations: millions of eggs by now, from Clatterbuck chickens into Coahoma homes. Dogs all over the Delta knew Will. Chained in yards or napping on porches, they might look up, but they never barked.

He loved his work, especially the gathering of the eggs. Whenever he entered his henhouses, it seemed to him that he had interrupted the chickens in secret, boisterous laughter, that their clucking was the quieting-down sound of fertile festivity.

As he carried the eggs to the door of Heartfield, he took in a newly furrowed field out back, a neat row of garbage cans nestled against the house, a strip of herb garden sweet with sage. He swung open the back door and went in, instinct leading him up a short, churchy-feeling hallway toward the kitchen. He smelled fresh-baked bread, a warm blooming scent that made him swing into the room with a smile. He saw:

Laughing men and women lifting loaves of bread from many ovens, ovens that snapped shut like startled mouths. The smell of bread sharpened into more scents: thyme, cinnamon, raisins. Swooping from oven to countertop, a half-dozen men and women bent over their baked bundles and inhaled deeply: "Ahhh." They spotted Will and froze where they stood, as still as deer.

"Here's your eggs," he said.

An efficient young woman bustled forward and made space on a butcher block counter. "Lovely. Put them right here, sir." To the others, she said, "Reverend Howard says we can have eggs!"

"You mean you haven't been eating them before?" Will said, addressing the group at large. Various faces—long, round, open, wary—regarded him, and he was glad he'd worn such a clean blue shirt. "Were you-all getting your eggs at the grocery store, or what?"

"None at all before today," the efficient woman said, counting the cartons that he'd stacked on the counter-top. "Eight dozen, nine dozen, ten dozen eggs." She and a stately older woman raised their arms and did a high-five. Facing Will with gratitude, the efficient young woman said, as if reciting from a book, "At Heartfield, we adhere to strict dietary guidelines. No alcohol, no tobacco, no meat, no sugar except honey. Up till now, no dairy. We don't have fruits and vegetables on the table at the same time. We bake fresh bread every day."

The older woman, serene as a queen, prompted her, "And now, Reverend Howard has said—"

"—has said eggs are all right," the young woman announced to Will. "He researched this. We're pretty excited about it." She looked around the group. The others relaxed; some smiled.

Will asked, "What do you do here? What kind of church is it?"

An earnest man with flour-dusted glasses plucked a brochure from his pocket and passed it to Will. "We practice physical and spiritual health. Really we're not much different from what you'd call mainstream denominations except that we're probably better cooks." The others laughed. The flour-stained glasses went on, "Have you heard about our detox program?"

Will shook his head, mesmerized by the man's easy, sonorous voice.

"Lots of executives come here to clean out their

systems," the man said. "Why, we get 'em from Jackson and Memphis and New Orleans. The smokers, we wrap those guys in sheets and steam 'em. You should see how yellow those sheets get when all the nicotine seeps out of their skin! There's a new bunch in the steam room right this minute. Newbies, we call them. Want to see 'em?"

"Now, Nelson," the queenly older woman said, with a quelling motion of her hands.

The man pushed his floury glasses up his nose and held out a loaf of bread. "For you and your family," he said. "I assume you've got a family."

"I have a wife. Thanks," Will said, tucking the bread under his arm.

"You and your wife must take a meal with us some time," the queenly lady said.

A girl threaded her way through the group, a solemn, fresh-faced redhead. "Come mushrooming with us," she said, "after the frosts are over. We'll find miracles."

"Morels, she means," said the floury glasses.

Will was suddenly afraid they would want to pray for him, would encircle him and touch him with pliant, yeasty hands. He backed out the door.

The red-haired girl followed him to his van. She called, "God spoke to us."

Will leaned out the van window and stared into her serious face. "What did God say?"

"We all heard Him," she said, "but what He said is a secret."

Will didn't mean to, but he sprayed gravel hard

against the shiny trash cans as he spun out of the parking lot.

He knew that Dulcie was ambivalent about kids. She wanted them aboard her bus in large numbers, fearing that a drop in enrollments would be the end of her job. Candidly critical, she regaled Will about which children had bad breath, which ones were ugly. Will defended them, pitying them; after all, didn't he help to nourish them, didn't they eat the eggs he delivered to their houses? Dulcie's pockets bulged with treats the children had given her: squirty blue bubblegum, monster-faced trading cards, plastic barrettes meant for baby-fine hair. It baffled Will, Dulcie's resistance to the children's affection. Maybe she simply resented the fact that her own daughters were dead, while these kids were so alive.

Long ago, Dulcie had been pregnant with twins. At seven months, her pains started. They raced to the hospital, where the doctor said, "You've got to keep them *in* longer. Stand on your head, by God." The nurses made Dulcie do just that, but it didn't work. The twins arrived so weak and tiny that they died in an incubator. Dulcie named them Jocelyn and Priscilla—sniffly, snuffly names that reminded Will of sneezes. Dulcie kept a photograph of them on the mantelpiece in the bedroom. Poor little things, they looked like chicks hatched too soon, so red and shut-eyed, too embryonic to be exposed to light and air. Every time Will looked at the picture, he expected to see bits of eggshell and yolk splattered on the twins' pink blankets and on their bald veined heads. They died even before he learned to tell them apart.

After their deaths, Dulcie began her job as a bus driver. Sometimes she would stop the bus and have a party in a field. She reported to Will that all of the children liked these impromptu stops except for Adam Smart, a six-year-old neighbor of theirs, who fussed that he would be late for school or late getting home. "He's got no spirit," Dulcie said. "No sense of fun."

Whatever Dulcie found on her bus, she kept. She cleaned it daily, combing the seat cushions and aisles for things left behind, collecting coins and pens and the occasional watch.

"If they ask me directly if I found something, I'll give it back," Dulcie would say. "Otherwise, finders, keepers."

"But they love you," Will said.

"You don't have to sound so surprised about it," said Dulcie.

Adam Smart, who worried about being on time, would be standing outside his house, down by the mailbox, early every morning. Dulcie received handmade cards from Adam Smart: "Dear Mrs. Clatterbuck, please don't stop the bus anymore." Defiantly, she slapped the notes up on the icebox door with fruit-shaped magnets. The magnets, too, were a gift from her riders.

Dulcie had nicknames for the children—names that disturbed Will: the Moppet, Goody Two-Shoes, the Gargoyle, the Three Little Pigs.

"That is so mean of you," he would tell her.

"I only tell the nicknames to you," she'd say, sounding stung. "I never call the kids that. I'm *not* mean." And she had the blue bubblegum and some new trading cards to prove it.

In all the years of delivering eggs, Will had rarely seen Dulcie driving her bus, though there were only a few roads in the county. When they did see one another, she'd give a signal that made him smile: her backscratcher brandished out the window in a high, wild salute, her horn pumping three shrill blasts. She drove too fast, and he told her so.

"The bus is my bronco," she'd say. "I know what it can and cannot do."

He hoped that one day he would come upon her having a party in a field. He pictured Dulcie and the children hopping off the golden bus and romping among cottonpatches and meadows of flowers or frost, sharing their candy and waving the colorful paper streamers that she kept in a basket beneath the driver's seat.

"I'm the best influence those kids will ever have," she liked to say. "All I want in this life is to keep on doing what I do."

Returning from his route, after that first day with Heartfield on the circuit, he found drama at home. Dulcie was in the yard when he pulled up, scanning the pearly horizon.

She called out to him, "My bloomers that we hung up this morning? They're gone, clothespins and all."

Will strode over and kissed her. Her mouth tasted of

green-apple jawbreakers. "Probably the wind took 'em off. They're probably caught in some trees, pretty as the clouds."

She shook her head. "There was not much wind today. Somebody stole them." She gazed toward Adam Smart's house, where distant smoke rose from the chimney. "I bet *he* took them, just to torment me. He always complains about the surprise parties. We had one yesterday, and he wouldn't even get off the bus."

"Adam wouldn't steal your bloomers," said Will. "You're too suspicious, Dulcie."

"The sheets are here. The towels, everything else is here, everything but the bloomers," she insisted, punching the pile of dry folded things in the laundry basket. "Somebody stole those bloomers to do nasty things with."

"There was a breeze this morning, don't you remember?" It seemed years ago they had stood on that spot, the bloomers puffing toward them in the daybreak wind. He felt tired: he was fifty-seven, the years slipping past him easy as an airborne sheet.

"I'll get them back, that's what I'll do." Dulcie headed down their driveway to the road.

He caught up with her. "You're going to accuse Adam Smart of stealing your bloomers?"

She glided away, tossing over her shoulder, "I made a meat loaf. Would you put it in the oven?"

She came back so late that the portion of meat loaf he'd saved for her was dry and hard. He was so angry he didn't look up when she came in.

She sat down at the table and dropped her head into her hands. "He didn't have them, or at least he claimed he didn't. His parents got real mad at me."

"I told you not to go. Dulcie, you are so damned sure that the world is out to do you wrong."

She was crying. "Let me be," she said.

"You can get another bathing suit, for Christ's sake."

"I don't think Adam's mad at me," she said, wiping her eyes. "He showed me his pet squirrel. He keeps it on top of a chest of drawers, with a little chain around its neck. It doesn't have anything to do except chew on the chest of drawers. You can see teeth marks all over the wood."

"Did you ask him if he stole the squirrel?" He was still disgusted, but he pushed the pan of dry meat loaf toward her.

"I asked him to let it go," she said, "but he said he loves it too much to do that."

On his second visit to Heartfield, he found the red-haired girl alone in the kitchen, leaning on the butcher block counter, reading a book. She looked up when he came in with the eggs and said, "I've just found this great recipe that uses bee pollen, raw cauliflower, and sunflower seeds."

Remembering a package of Twinkies in his jacket pocket, he pulled it out and gave it to her. "Have some real food."

"Reverend Howard would kill me!" She shuddered prettily, sniffing the cakes through the cellophane.

"Where did you live before you came here?" Will asked her. The silence around them made him alert; he smelled the faint perfume of gas from the cool stoves.

"I've lived in a lot of places. Florida, the Ivory Coast, Spain," the girl said, blinking her gray eyes slowly. "In Spain I saw a bullfight. The matador cut out the bull's heart and gave it to me."

"Are you being kept here against your will?" Will said. "Does Reverend Howard control the people here?"

The girl laughed, her body jiggling in a fluid line. "Don't talk crazy. This is practically a health club. We can do anything we want. Besides, Reverend Howard is my father. Kind of my father; he's my mother's boyfriend. He's out blessing the new herbs we planted."

Will leaned against the counter, welcoming the reassurance.

The girl said, "A bat got in last night, and guess who got rid of it—me. I went and fetched our long-handled net and caught it and let it out again. A lot of the guys were scared of it. They ran into their rooms yelling and slammed the doors." She chuckled.

"Where's everybody else now?"

"Oh, meditating or exercising."

He stood up tall and straight, full of the proud knowledge that he could rescue her if she needed it. She regarded him as if he were quite presentable, though he knew how he looked—all big shoes, lank gray-brown hair, and stupid smile. "There's some double yolks in there," he told her, pointing at the eggs he'd brought.

"You have a special talent with egg-farming," she

said. "I can tell. One of the things we do here is develop everybody's special talents."

"What's yours?" He felt his face flush.

"I'll show you." She opened a cupboard over the sink, lifted out several drinking glasses, filled them halfway with water, and set them on the counter. She licked her fingertips and ran them around the edges of the glasses.

The thin tumblers sang with clear, high sounds. Will watched her flying hands, her fingers coaxing melody from the shining rims of the glasses. He was caught by the odd sweet music, more beautiful than anything he'd heard on the radio or in church—bright, bell-toned, humming haloes. The very air took on spangly rainbow colors.

As the last tones melted away, she said, "I'm saving money to buy a harp."

"You ought to be on TV," Will said.

"I've been on TV already, back when I was a little kid," she said, flicking a fingernail against one of the glasses. "A person can always get better with their special talent."

Some days later, the radio in his van brought him news of an accident. A school bus had run off the road, crashing into a pecan grove that had been ruined by the ice storm, hurling all of the children from their seats. The local hospital had filled up with them, the broadcaster said: three with broken bones, one with a concussion, many more with bad bruises.

He knew—he knew it was Dulcie. Flooring the van, he raced home. Ambulance workers had tried to take Dulcie, too, to the hospital, but she refused, doctoring herself at home. She wore a wide bandage across her forehead and greeted Will irritably.

"The school superintendent came by to insult me," she reported. "He said Adam Smart told him I wasn't looking at the road, that I was rubbing myself under my clothes. I asked him, Since when is using a back-scratcher against the law? He put me on a leave of absence. I bet he gives my route to Lena Wickham."

"Dulcie, tell me how the accident happened."

"A UFO is what happened," Dulcie said. "It came bursting out of the clouds and landed right on my fender. It was so bright that I couldn't see anything else, so I went off the road into the trees."

"Who's going to believe that? Next you'll say Lena Wickham was riding on the UFO."

"I'm sticking to the facts," she insisted, her face composed and blank. "Cows across the road saw it, too. They followed it with their eyes."

"Whatever happened, just tell me. Did you look away from the road for a second? Is something wrong with the bus? Maybe the steering—"

She cut him off. "That superintendent didn't believe me, but you're my husband. You have to believe me."

"Dulcie, you know you like to exaggerate. Was the sun reflecting off the fender? Was that the bright light you saw?"

"Today was cloudy," she said.

"You need your rest," he told her, and led her to their bedroom. She wouldn't lie down, just sat at her dressing table winding a green scarf over the bandage on her head.

"Well, I'm worn out," Will said. He lay down and closed his eyes. Soft darkness settled in the room. "I don't understand you, Dulcie."

The bed shifted with her weight as she eased down beside him. He opened his eyes and saw her gazing at him. She said, "Why did Adam Smart lie about me? I never did anything to him. I miss that bus. It's at some garage, being fixed. Just love me." She buried her head against his stomach with a force that knocked the breath out of him.

When he woke the next morning, she wasn't there. He had overslept, and the high sun made pleats of light on the bedroom walls.

The van was gone. The cartons of eggs which the previous night he had neatly stacked in coolers by the chickenhouse door, ready for loading, were missing too.

He asked a neighbor to drive him around. They caught up with Dulcie near the school. She pulled over and waited, as if Will and the neighbor were police officers who would issue her a ticket.

Will trotted to the van and peered over Dulcie's shoulder. "Good Lord," he said. Sunbursts of eggs festooned the inside of the van, their broken yolks and sticky whites dripping and oozing gelatinously from the seat, the walls, the steering wheel. Ragged shells clung to the dashboard.

"I hit a bump," Dulcie explained, waving her hand, "and a bunch of them went flying. You didn't have them packed very good."

"Have you lost your mind?" Will cried. He signaled to the neighbor to go on home.

"I tried to wake you up this morning," she said. "If the customers don't get their eggs, we'll lose business. I picked up some of my riders, too. The kids helped me remember which houses to deliver to. Then I took them to school."

"Move over," Will said, and she slid over so that he could get in behind the steering wheel. The van smelled terrible, all yolk and albumen, a raw slick stench.

"It was fun going into everybody's houses," Dulcie said. "Plus, that Heartfield place is pretty interesting. We ate omelettes there, and a redheaded girl played music on water-glasses. Where are we going?"

"To see a doctor," Will said.

"There is nothing wrong with me," said Dulcie in a reasonable voice, and that was what the doctor said, too, after examining her: "Nothing wrong here," as if the egg-splattered van out in the parking lot were proof of Dulcie's well-being.

The telephone shrilled at them from the moment they got home. Outraged parents cried, "You are *not* supposed to drive my kids around in an egg van! And why are my eggs all broken this time? There's not a single good one in the bunch."

That night, Will couldn't sleep. He kept picturing the van careening around the roads, full of lurching children, eggs hurtling and cracking, and Dulcie blithely stepping into the quiet houses to leave boxes of ruined eggs on kitchen counters. Beside him, Dulcie snored in a pitch halfway between a growl and a purr.

So he was still awake when, at midnight, he heard a knock on the back door. He grabbed his robe, padded downstairs, and peered through the glass window of the back door. Smiling on the steps, his face white beneath the security light, was the man in floury glasses, bundled up in a parka and waving Dulcie's backscratcher.

As Will opened the door, the night air burst in coldly, smelling of wild onions.

"This is your wife's, I believe," the man said, handing the backscratcher to Will. "I found it tonight when I cleaned up the kitchen. She paid us a lovely visit. We think very highly of Dulcie." The man's nostrils looked icy, and Will saw with amazement that he had arrived on a bike.

"Come in," he said, remembering the man's name: the queenly lady at Heartfield had called him Nelson.

The man unzipped his parka and sat down in the living room, rubbing his hands together. "I'd love a hot cuppa, but not tea or coffee. Do you have any Ovaltine? And well, not to put you to any trouble, but maybe a bite to eat. Pizza, if you've got it. That was quite a ride! It's exactly five miles from here to Heartfield. I clocked it."

"You could have kept that backscratcher until I came

by with your eggs," Will said. "I mean thanks, but there wasn't any hurry."

"Oh, but there was," the man said merrily. "Dulcie's crazy about that little thing. Yes, she came by this morning with the eggs and a bunch of schoolkids, and we had a real party."

When Will got back from the kitchen with a mug of hot chocolate and a peanut butter sandwich, the TV set was on.

"*Petticoat Junction,*" the man said. "I used to love this show. Imagine three gorgeous sisters living at a railroad station. Be still, my heart!" He gulped the cocoa and bit deeply into the sandwich. "We don't allow TV at Heartfield, of course."

Will eased himself onto the sofa. It's my house, he reminded himself, yet everything looked unfamiliar—the cold, ashy fireplace, the broken cuckoo clock, the floor lamp with the embroidered shade. The man's glasses were so floury that Will could not see his eyes. "What's your full name?" he asked him.

"Nelson Archibald." The man pointed to the TV. "After all these years, I can still tell them apart—Bobbie Jo, Betty Jo, and my favorite, Billie Jo."

"I have to get up real early," Will said. He wanted this person to go.

"Of course you do," said Nelson Archibald. He pulled an envelope from his pocket. "This letter is from Reverend Howard to your wife. He could tell she's in distress. It's a personal invitation for her to come to Heartfield and stay as long as she likes."

"Mind your own business."

Nelson Archibald laid the letter on Will's knees. "Hey, it's just meant in friendship." He slipped into his parka and swept out the door. Through the window, Will watched the bicycle gleam down the long driveway, its headlamp cutting a path through the night.

Dulcie's voice startled him. "Hey, Will?" she said, and he whipped around to see her coming down the stairs, barefoot. "I heard what he said. I might take them up on that invitation."

"Don't even consider going, Dulcie. Can't you eat health food and say prayers right here at home? You're not even religious."

"Heartfield isn't about religion, really. I liked those people." She pointed to the backscratcher. "That was sweet of Nelson to bring it to me."

"Especially in the middle of the night, to wake us up." Will picked up the backscratcher and tapped its tiny curved hand on his palm. The wooden fingers felt personal and distinct, strong enough to gouge out his eyes. He flexed the handle.

"Don't, you'll break it," Dulcie said.

Even as Will snapped it in two and threw the pieces down, he was sorry. The little hand looked forlorn on the floor, and Dulcie's cry was sharp.

"It's just a toy," he said.

On the TV screen, Betty Jo, Bobby Jo, and Billie Jo did the can-can for the benefit of passengers stepping off a train. Will reached over and clicked the TV set off, knocking over Nelson Archibald's mug. Cocoa dregs left a scallop of dark stain on the carpet.

The mess made him domestic. He hurried to the kitchen to get a clean-up cloth from the rag bag that Dulcie kept beneath the sink. That was where he found her bloomers, wadded up with old shreds of flannel and calico scented with lemon furniture oil—the frilly white bloomers, split at the seams.

"Those bloomers," Dulcie said when she saw them in his hand. "I finally found them tangled up in one of the sheets. They're too small for me now." She tore a strip of cloth from the bloomers and pressed it against the spill, dabbing the cocoa out of the carpet.

He said, "Here, let me do that."

Dulcie didn't answer him. Absorbed in her work, she stretched out on the rug like a bathing beauty sunning herself on sand. Their living room might have been a beach, and Will, bending over her, might have been an umbrella, or a palm tree, or a man who hoped to make her acquaintance.

Manna from the Sky

THERE'S A chicken factory near here and that's what smells so bad. On the highway, look for the big trucks that carry the chickens to their death-place. They're crammed into tiers of wire cages, thousands to a truck, feathers flattened by the wind, and if you catch the eye of any chicken, prostrate with despair or simply squashed from rocketing along at sixty miles an hour, you will see intelligence in that yellow eye; you can tell that the chicken knows where it's going and is not happy about it. At the factory, cranes unload the stacks of crates from the big trucks, lowering the chickens onto a conveyor belt that whisks them into the plant. They'll come out as roasters or fryer parts or neat little palm-sized pieces that you can cut up and stir-fry. What happens to all the feathers? Pillows? And the blood goes to lipstick companies, right?

But this story isn't just about chickens. It's about

how one person leads to another. It's about a mother and father and their son Stanley, an all-white child. His skin and hair were so pale that he looked like he should never go out in the sun, though he wasn't an albino, just a shade or two away from that. And poor Stanley had breasts that quivered beneath his T-shirts so that he kept his arms folded across his chest when the teacher made the children run relays. Put your arms down, Stanley, the teacher would holler, you'll run faster, and she made him put his arms down, and then everybody saw how his breasts jigged up and down, and they tormented him in his misery.

His mother and father ran a drugstore—his father was the pharmacist and his mother tended the lunch counter and did everything else too, like wrapping presents when customers wanted some little knick-knack gift-wrapped, a picture frame or a vase or a stuffed animal or a box of stale candy. The wrapping paper was plain and cheap and old, in rolls so big the pharmacist said they'd never have to worry about buying more.

Even though the parents worked hard all day, they stayed up late every night in their apartment over the shop. At three in the morning the mother would glide into the kitchen in her robe and get snacks of cheese crackers or canned peaches or whatever was left over from supper, and she'd sit around reading the paper or folding laundry, and the father would remember something he had to do in the store and he'd go downstairs and unlock the door, and always somebody'd see the lights on and bang on the door to please be let in so they could buy cough syrup or painkiller or some prescription for a relative who was about to die for sure. And how could the father say no?

The child lived like his parents did, snacking late and rambling around the house with a sandwich in his hand, playing with his toys, opening and shutting the windows, puttering around till he fell asleep from exhaustion on the couch or in his bed.

Everybody in the family had trouble getting up in the morning, so the boy suffered not only from his paleness and his breasts but also from the stigma of tardiness. His schoolmates held their shirts out from their chests with thumbs and forefingers, saying, "Oh my! Late again! I was just playing with my boobs and missed the bus." The boy would not tell his parents about the taunting; he was too proud and besides, even though he was only eleven he could see they had problems enough. Saturday mornings he helped his father in the store and saw him groggily flick pills into bottles, saw his mother commit a hundred absent-minded sins against hygiene—mopping the floor with the same rag she used to swab the lunch counter, getting the spoons for tuna salad and her own coffee cup mixed up, serving coffee to a customer in the cup she'd been drinking from herself. It was the coffee that saved the family, day after day, though it took till noon to wake them up for real.

The child, hunched over at one end of the counter gulping from a chipped cup, looked oddly grown-up.

His daddy passed by him and ran a hard thumb down his back and cried, "Sit up straight, Stanley. You're so bent over, your spine's gunna warp," and that thumb pressed so hard on Stanley's spine that Stanley gagged on his hot coffee and spilled it all over his shirt. Then his mother fussed and sighed, and Stanley developed the nervous habit of pulling on his arm hair, which was long, and twisting it up into little points. He was nervous, but he was smart, and soon he could do all kinds of things, like operate the cash register and stock the shelves and sweep the floors, and his parents came to rely on him. Now and again on a Saturday they'd sleep a little later and send Stanley downstairs to open the shop. He could do lots of things, except of course fool with medicine, could serve food and wrap gifts and make change.

This was in North Carolina, where it gets so hot in the summertime and stays boiling way into fall, and on those hot days, that chicken factory just stank, smelled like guts and gore and awful vile parts and deeds. When the wind was right, the smell swept through town and got all mixed up with the stale smell of the air conditioning in the drugstore, so the family went around with their noses looking pinched all the time. The father would tell the mother, "Aren't you lucky I married you, otherwise you'd still be working at the plant with a shower-cap on your head," and she'd snap, "It was good money. Mr. Rice says I can have my job back anytime," and her husband would say, "As if he knows who you are."

Who was Mr. Rice, that they fought about him? He was a chicken legend who had started out in that very town with a backyard flock of Wyandottes and Rhode Island Reds and had built up a chicken empire. He was old, but he still went after women. Nobody in town ever saw him, because he was so famous that he didn't have to live anywhere at all except on the pages of magazines. His mother still lived in that little town, though, in an ordinary house with dirty windows and stumps in the front yard. Mr. Rice's admirers said he was mean and smart; his enemies said he was mean and stupid. All anybody could agree on was that he was damn rich.

Stanley heard his parents fuss, picked up on the undercurrents, and tried to be extra-good. Whenever he wanted to do a bad thing, he resisted. When other children stood on their front porches spraying passing cars with hard blasts from garden hoses, or scrambled over wet cement writing bad words, or scooped dog shit into paper bags and set the bags afire and left them on people's porches to be stomped out by the unwary—when other children did that kind of thing, Stanley was just good, and when the other children came to the store and teased him, always out of earshot of his mother and father, he didn't say a word, just grew pale red like the mark that a stinging nettle leaves on skin.

A person was disturbing the lives of his father and mother, a woman who was new in town: a female undertaker, broad-shouldered and pale-lashed with a knowing gaze. Her funeral parlor was just a few blocks from the drugstore and she let it be known that she had paid cash for the business. She went to the barber every two weeks so that her hair was short as a man's, downright military, and she kept a little jar of Jervis powder in her pocket and clapped powder on the back of her neck on hot days as she sat up at the lunch counter. Men liked her. They'd joke, "How's business? Bet it's dead," and she'd laugh and pass a hand over her short hair and say, "Seriously, guys, don't be afraid of me," and she'd give a monster-laugh like in the movies, *heeaaugh!* that would set everybody at the lunch counter to rocking and guffawing, everybody except Stanley's mother. Stanley'd cut his eyes over to his mother's set jaw, and he'd put the same look on his own face.

But Stanley's father made a big fuss over the undertaker, whose name was Sarah (Serra, as people said it). "Serra, for somebody that works with dead folks, you're the livingest person I know," and she'd put her big square hand on his arm and say, "Thanks, darlin'. I'll save my nicest box for ya," and Stanley's father, who'd never had much to do with the lunch counter crowd before, now crowed, "Hey fellas, y'all hear that?"

"Don't talk to me anymore. I'm reading," she'd say, holding up a page of obits in front of her face. "Departed this life—" and she'd say the name of whoever was sitting next to her, while the laughter started and kept on coming. Stanley's father, who never let anybody read newspapers or magazines without buying them first, let Sarah read anything she wanted. So she read comic books, *Field and Stream, Motor Trend,* anything.

She baited Stanley's mother. "Your son can have a

job with me. I'll teach him all there is to know, from the totin' in to the layin' out to the diggin' and layin' in," and Stanley's mother said, real mad, "I'd rather see him dead than be an undertaker," and that broke up the lunch counter, and when Stanley's mother realized her pun, she slapped her rag on the counter and turned her back on Sarah.

The mother and father fought about Sarah, in the long nights while they puttered around the apartment. Stanley's mother said, "She ought to be run out of town, so unnatural and bold about it. When I die, she's not getting her hands on me," and Stanley's father said, "She's got joy in her, a heap more than you ever had. You don't know a thing about her."

Then Sarah started reading another kind of magazine at the lunch counter: girlie magazines. Yes, the kind you had to ask Stanley's father for at the cash register, because he kept them underneath the shelf. She kept the covers folded back, so that when men asked, "What're you readin', Serra?" she'd flash the cover at them, a full-color shot of big bare bosoms hanging out of a bathing suit—and while the men reeled with shock, she'd read aloud: "Dear Sirs, Let me tell you about something my girlfriend and I have discovered that is really wonder-ful—" and then she'd break off and slap her thigh and the men would say, "Jeez-*um*."

Stanley's mother stopped that right quick, snatch-ing the girlie magazines out of Sarah's hands: "Get out," and Sarah groaned, "Blondie" (for that was her nickname for Stanley's mother), "where's your sense of fun?" and sauntering to the doorway, she blew kisses to everyone at the lunch counter.

Soon she was back, reading just sports magazines again. One day, while Stanley was arranging stuffed animals in a bin at the end of an aisle, Sarah said, "How'd you like to come by my place for a look-see?"

"No thanks," he said. A blue bunny rabbit spun out of his grasp, and Sarah retrieved it with a grin.

He didn't go to her funeral parlor, but he thought about what she'd said. He got so tired of feeling alone all the time. In the long sleeve of the purple nights, as he fumbled among his toys or sat in front of the oscillating fan eating fried pork rinds, he traveled to Sarah's funeral parlor in his mind. Long nights went by that way. The town was silent and dark except for the lights of the chicken factory, which ran twenty-four hours a day and cared nothing about midnight or noon. Oh, it was hot, and the oscillating fan, breezing right and left in the dark at Stanley, never lingered long enough on his face to cool him, was always aiming its blessing somewhere else.

As if Sarah hadn't changed things enough, her sister came to town, or at least a woman that Sarah said was her sister. There was no physical resemblance, nor any likeness in the way they behaved. The sister was much younger than Sarah, just a girl really, and her name was December. She had been paralyzed for many years, Sarah said, able to move nothing but her eyes, and when the paralysis lifted, by a miracle nobody could explain, she grew strong and lovely. And yes, she was lovely: her face became the light that Stanley lived by, that beautiful sad face with straight dark brows and the sad proud lift of her chin.

But unlike Sarah, who talked all the time, December hardly said a word. And soon a tale began to creep around town: that she had a secret, a something in her that made her lust after many men, all men. She could not help it; it was something in her head or her body or both that put the lusting beyond her control. Men: old or young or ugly or fine, it didn't matter, and having them only made her want them more. Was it true? Or was it just a myth, sprung from the heat waves and the boiling clouds that would not rain, that hung heavy as mince pie over the town?

By day, December sat on a swiveling stool at the lunch counter and looked at her hands. Men had given her bracelets and rings. She wore wonderful clothes— green leather boots, gold suede dresses, beaded belts and silver sashes. If Sarah, with her rough funny talk and her girlie magazines, had been a torment to Stanley's mother, December, with her beauty and silence and wildness, was a curse.

Once, needing toothpaste, Stanley crept barefoot down to the drugstore around three in the morning, and there were his father and December twisting and turning on the floor in between the shelves of mouthwash and shampoo. Stanley thought he heard his mother whisper, "Be a statue," so he stood very still, just a few yards from where they lay. But his mother wasn't there, and the only sounds were the choppy chants that

his father and December were making. Clothes were
all over the place. One of his father's shoes had landed
on a shelf, knocking bottles of hair-dye and tubes of
mustache-wax into a jumble. Stanley noticed how
scuffed and creased that shoe was. It needed a new lace.

He watched them, thinking how hard the floor was,
and then on stiff tip-toes ran pell-mell past the familiar
smells of coffee grinds at the lunch counter and witch-
hazel at the make-up shelf. Two at a time, he took the
steps that led to the apartment.

He kept thinking about his father's shoe, so worn-
out that the heel and toe had no dye on them at all, and
tried to remember where the polish was kept. He fell
asleep trying.

One day, the famous chicken man came into the
drugstore. Yes, Mr. Rice! He was alone, though everybody had thought he used bodyguards. But it was him,
all long-legged stride and blue eyes and so what if
he was old, all that money kept alive a fire in his eyes
that was triumph. His car, black as an oil slick, purred
double-parked outside the store. He went to the cash
register, where Stanley's mother was cracking cylinders
of pennies into the penny compartment, and called her
by name.

"Florie, Florie, do you remember me?"

She drew a hand across her forehead and swayed, unable to speak.

"A box of candy is what I want, candy for my
mother," he said, and Stanley's mother, like a wound-

up toy, scurried to the candy shelf cooing, "This one? This one?" and Mr. Rice smiled and said, "Any one you pick is fine with me," and in her distraction, Stanley's mother wrapped up the display box, which wasn't candy at all, but plastic—plastic nougats and butter-creams and Jordan almonds.

Mr. Rice spotted December poised at the lunch counter, dunking her rings into a water glass to clean them. She slid off the stool and came toward him, her arms outstretched. It was that easy.

"Well, who are *you?*" the chicken man asked, but she didn't need to say a word. Mr. Rice snatched the box of candy from Stanley's mother, forgetting even to pay for it, and with December on his arm, he pegged out the door, into the heat, and into his big black car.

That night, Mr. Rice's mother ate the plastic candy and died from it. What excitement there was all over town, and how proud Sarah was to lay the old lady out in a casket lined with eggplant-colored satin. At the funeral, Mr. Rice clasped December around the waist and didn't hide the joy on his face; his mother's death didn't matter one whit, now that he had December.

Stanley was watching December and Mr. Rice. Once, when he was very young, his parents had taken him to a park to see swans. They were beautiful, lovely and white and shaped like graceful teapots. Their slow, windy wings thrilled him. To one of them, he held out a piece of broken toast. Closer, closer: he could see the tiny holes in the gold beak, the holes it breathed through. But it was mean, it bit him. The mean swan . . . the mean swan . . . he remembered the swan as he looked at December standing tall and still in Mr. Rice's arms. The swan hadn't known what it was doing, and maybe December didn't either.

Now think about something in your own life, so you'll understand how Stanley felt. Think about that time when your heart was wide open, when you had just whispered to someone, "I love you," and you knew if they didn't say it back, your heart would crack in two. Up to that point, it was just you, your own self, and now all of a sudden you were in love. Your beloved's face floated before you all the time, turning your heart to quicksand and tuning wild fiddles in your blood.

Stanley stood there with his wide-open heart. His parents and the townspeople were there too, in that flat graveyard with the familiar names carved into the stones, but all he could think about was December. Her wild eyes fluttered over him. He could tell she didn't care about Mr. Rice's mother.

It was sunset, and the children of the town, weary from waiting all day for the funeral, turned their restless attention to new amusement and focused on Stanley, standing at the graveside in serious black clothes. He held a cap to his chest to cover it. He hoped it would soon be dark, so his thoughts would be ever more his own. But as the mourners left the graveyard, the children surrounded Stanley. They taunted him with buzzing, yelping sentences that came at him too fast to contradict. They started touching him, grabbing him and twisting his sensitive breasts, in a horrible way that was meant to hurt. Stanley flailed at them with his fists. There were girls as well as boys, mocking and persecuting and hurling him to the ground. He cried out and fought back as hard as he could, but the adults, milling here and there about the graveyard, didn't seem to notice at all.

Except December. All of a sudden she was there beside him, bending over and shielding him from his attackers. He tasted dirt in his mouth and his chest stung from the blows and the pinches, and above him was December's white moon-face with the straight black eyebrows. So fierce were the other children, that they hit her too, before they realized what they were doing and pulled back from her afraid. December drew Stanley close to her so that they were sitting awkwardly on a plot of grass next to a stone that said, "Our Lamb." Stanley knew a happiness that he'd never known before, there in the arms of that strange silent woman who had rescued him.

He didn't hear her words, but her pale straight lips moved. Beyond her shoulder, he saw the brown-shod feet of his classmates clumping away. He thought again of his father's scuffed shoe in the aisle of the store, and he cried.

December lifted his shirt and kissed his bare bruised flesh, his tender harried chest. His tears heated his head like a furnace.

Next, something happened that made the death of Mr. Rice's mother seem, in comparison, like a card party. The very night of the funeral, December was back in the drugstore with Stanley's father, and they didn't bother to turn off the lights. Mr. Rice's black car came snarling down the street, slowed and idled in front of the store, and Mr. Rice smashed open the glass door and strode in and tore the two apart from each other, as Stanley watched frozen from behind the bin of stuffed animals.

Then Mr. Rice shot—yes, shot—Stanley's father, while December, naked, backed slowly up the aisle, ran out the door, and hopped into Mr. Rice's car. Her dress, a shirred gold sheath, lay near Stanley's feet like a bright caterpillar, the scent of Houbigant seeping out of it like a sly soul arising and sneaking for Heaven's door. Stanley had come downstairs that time to get some Mercurochrome for his mother, who had cut her leg while shaving and had sent him to the store, scolding him for not wanting to go.

His mother, having heard the gunshot, came tumbling down the stairs in her nightgown, her loose hair spiraling across her forehead, and cried to Mr. Rice, "I'll never forgive you. My hate will follow you everywhere."

So there was more business for Sarah, a box for Stanley's father and a sweet dark grave in the graveyard, and lots of different versions of the story flying here and there among the flat streets of the town and among the chicken plant workers as they stripped the pinfeathers from the limp yellow bodies and pried the gizzards loose from the inside.

Mr. Rice went to jail for awhile, but now he's out

again, richer than ever. Sarah says she knows where December is but won't tell, "Because she's my sister and I love her." Stanley's mother still runs the drugstore; why not, it's profitable enough, and people are still so curious about what happened that they come in and buy things. The children who had tormented Stanley got older and were tormented by problems of their own.

All this was a long time ago, so long that when you go back to wherever you yourself grew up, your old house is small and shabby and your childhood playmates are long since aged and married two or three times over. Love and hate and jealousy have changed them and changed you, too.

You're saying, I bet Stanley became a preacher. A child like that, watching fornication in a drugstore, seeing his daddy shot, would either grow up to kill people his own self, or else spend his whole lifetime running after Jesus, just to grasp the hem of His robe. Well no, he didn't become a preacher. He stayed at the drugstore, working hard. His breasts dropped right off him. Went from short and fat to tall and lean, with a look in his eye that stopped questions before they could get out of people's mouths.

Stanley has a question of his own. He'll spring it on you anytime, when you're dumping Sweet 'n Low into your coffee or gripping your gut begging him to hurry with that prescription for stomach flu. He'll fix you with his hard pale eyes and say, "What if everybody you'd ever been mad at was laying dead in a ditch, and you had the power to bring one of them back to life, who would it be? Do you have the name in your head? Fine—now just think about it. You've forgiven that person and brought them back from the dead, but they're sure—just sure—to cross you again, and then think how mad you'd be. You'd feel double-betrayed and wish you'd left them laying in the ditch with all the others."

Whenever he asks you that, no matter how hot a day it is, you'll feel cold inside. Why, you'd be so mad to be double-double-crossed, you'd probably die of your own rage. You'd say to that person: "To think I let you *live!*" and then you'd keel over from being angry. What is that word in the Bible—smite? smote? You'd be smitten, but in the bad way (which means death), and not in the good way, which means to fall in love.

The Girl Who Died in a Dance Marathon

I first encountered the marathoners in 1932 at The Palace of Wasted Footsteps in Freeport, Illinois . . .
—GEORGE EELS, "SOME 20,000 WERE IN 'MARATHON DANCE' BIZ AT ZENITH OF CRAZE," VARIETY, 7 JANUARY 1970

INSTANTLY, ON the schooner, Jane felt a connection with the little boy. Slipshod, he ran from side to side of the boat as tourists crammed against the rails and searched the gray horizon for the whales' distant plumes of steam. Jane watched as the boy jockeyed for a place to see. She murmured to her husband, "Is he with anyone? He seems so unparented."

Jane: a young woman, once provincial, who thanks to her husband had seen far more of the world than she ever expected. The little boy: aged nine, son of divorced parents, determined to stay as far as possible away from

141

his diminutive, punitive father, his guardian for this trip.

Jane's husband said, "He seems to be all by himself."

"What would that be like?" she said, knowing that this was the last vacation they would take together. The marriage, they had agreed for months, was over, yet moments sustained them, made it hard to let go. The little boy's aloneness stoked the bond between them.

A third person could do that, Jane reflected. She remembered their trip to Paris. Walking down the sidewalk, holding hands, intent on their conversation (they had just seen a movie, and movies always absorbed them), she had felt her husband's hand grow cold in hers. Paying no attention, they strolled on together, until laughter surrounded them, laughing faces like luminaria all along the Paris street. Turning around, she discovered a mime creeping along behind them, his hand on their clasped hands. It was the mime's cold fingers she had mistaken for her husband's. The mime had made them part of his act. Jane's heart pounded. Her husband's face was startled, young-looking, as he decided to laugh, too. The mime slipped into the darkness, his white-painted cheeks as bright as his teeth.

Now they were in Canada—far away from the southern city where they made their home—in Canada, out on the Bay of Fundy, where she had begged to go ever since the early days of their seven-year marriage, invoking the legend of the high tides. Fundy: where the whales lived. And the little boy was there, and the other tourists, shapeless in their sweatshirts and sun visors, maddening pushy people, Americans all. Bet they don't know where Ottawa is, Jane thought. Or Manitoba. God knows, even Montreal.

A heavy young woman sat astern. It was she who had organized the expedition, she who instructed the peering baygoers about the marine life they hoped to see. She gave slide shows every evening at an inn on Grand Manan Island. Holder of many degrees, a biologist of repute despite her youth, expert on right whales, she spoke in the low, melodic voice that Jane associated, surprisingly, with overweight people. Patiently the large woman answered the same questions each evening, as the guests of the inn wanted to know, How much does a whale weigh? How long do they live? The woman's knowledge showed in her vocabulary. She explained about baleen, which substituted for teeth, and about colossities, the barnaclelike formations crowning the whales' heads, as singular as fingerprints.

Now, placid on her high seat beside the ship's captain, she nibbled a cracker. Jane had made terrible fun of the biologist to her husband, yet she respected her knowledge, her concern about the whales. Jane was curious about the woman's life, which seemed so self-sufficient, driven by science. Jane believed that most lives were transparent. A careful eye could lay bare a life's motives and yearnings. Jane often analyzed her friends' lives, guessing secrets so accurately that her husband professed amazement. Now she turned her gaze on the woman as if on a crystal ball. There she sits like a caliph, Jane thought.

"Look!" someone cried, and the tourists raced to one side of the boat.

"Porpoises," the biologist said. Her binoculars gave her a distant, superior aspect that irritated Jane. Envy seeped through her: clearly the woman liked her life. She was making a difference. She had power: she could organize people, take charge, call up the captain of this boat and say let's go. Sit next to the captain and talk with him, man to man.

"There's a whale!"

The summons, sounded by a vigorous old lady standing astern, brought everyone to one side of the boat, cameras firing away. The whale was magnificent. It surfaced, blew, breached (Jane knew from the biologist's lecture that this meant leaping—soaring across the gray waves as if in joy), and finally dove (hundreds of feet, the biologist said they could go), waving its flukes tantalizingly above the surface before disappearing.

"That was wonderful," sighed a woman at Jane's elbow, and Jane turned with an automatic smile. The woman was about her age, with two toddlers and a baby. Chatting, they discovered they both lived in Florida. The woman's sister had attended Jane's college but no, Jane did not know her.

"They let you bring the kids on board?" Jane asked,

hiding her annoyance. The baby fussed, and the toddlers fretted underfoot. The mother seemed exhausted.

"The captain said as long as my husband and I watch them, it's OK." She jerked her chin starboard. "My husband's back there. The kids wear him out."

Jane's husband appeared and Jane introduced him. He leaned down, hands on knees, and said jovially to a toddler, "Did you see the big whale?"

The child squinted, drooling. Jane turned away, familiar anger shaking her chest. I can't do it, she thought, I can't bear to have a baby, and it's not fair to him. It has done us in. It should be such a simple thing.

Jane's husband, Kenneth, took his handkerchief and wiped the drool from the child's chin. The child's mother smiled weakly. The smile made crow's feet spread from the corners of her eyes. Jane touched her own face. Her skin was firm and uncreased, thanks to sunblock, sunglasses, and hats.

The other woman read her mind. Shifting the baby in her arms, she said, "I don't care if I get sunburn today. I used to drench myself in iodine and baby oil and just bake. Now I know that kind of thing—"

"—can absolutely destroy skin," said Jane. Kenneth shot her a startled glance.

"Mine's gone," said the young mother cheerfully. "Yours is beautiful."

"Thank you," said Jane, ashamed. Her husband used to tease her about never passing a mirror without looking at herself. Now he checked mirrors too. Both of them were obsessed with youth, young still but

tormented by time galloping, needy and unable to supply the other's needs, their marriage a flat dry place they
kept crossing, jauntily, conscious always of how they
looked to the world.

Jane, a high school teacher, had done a terrible thing
at the end of the last semester. She put the students'
exams away unread and marked down anything she
wanted on the final grade sheet. She raced down the list,
filling in ABCDF in seconds, sparing herself that te-
dious reading of essays, that agony of deciding border-
line cases. She turned in the grades and spent the rest of
the afternoon seeing if her breasts were big enough to
hold a pencil beneath them (one was, one almost was).
She laughed to herself as she tucked the pencil in place,
the same pencil she had used on the grade tally.

Now, more than a thousand miles from school,
where no one could find her, guilt rose up to choke her.
She thought with remorse of all the time that the students had put into the exams and of her failure to respond to that effort. Why, she could be fired, should be
fired. Kenneth, when she had told him what she had
done, had been horrified, then silent.

"Can't you laugh for once?" she said. "You act like
I'm so dreadful, everything I do."

"Our plane tickets arrived," he said, slapping them
down on the table.

Jane seized the tickets. "Grand Manan," she said.
"Fundy Bay. We'll have fun, won't we?"

"I hope so," he said, in a tone that indicated he could not possibly have fun with her again.

It had been half an hour since the last whale was sighted. After the initial glory of the one that breached, the hopeful tourists were rewarded with the sight of a mother and calf (the biologist had taught them that the Bay of Fundy was a nursery for mothers and calves, precious resources since only three hundred right whales remained in the world—the entire world, Jane thought with wonder and sadness). They were far from land. The water met the sky. Jane thought how the boat could keel over in a storm, carry them to the cold dark bottom where only the whales would go. With her last breath she would cry Kenneth, I love you, I love you. It was not her heart that would speak so much as her mind, her intentions, the promise she had made years before and kept with increasing resentment, as unable to leave him as he was to leave her. Their friends complimented them on their happiness, the way they always arrived at parties hand in hand, their smiles eager as children's. Marking time, waiting for whatever would set them free. Break them out, or take them to the bottom of the sea.

Lunch was served. Jane congratulated herself that, thanks to a Dramamine tablet, she could eat despite the increasingly heavy rolling of the boat. A barefoot, wild-haired boy—the first mate—scrambled up from the galley with a pot of steaming clam chowder, thick with potatoes and onions, and a platter of cold cuts. Gulping the soup from a mug, Jane grew aware of someone at her elbow: the unparented boy, his brown eyes bright and pleading as an animal's, and instinctively Jane fed him.

"Here, have some chowder." She pushed a mug into his hands. "What's your name?"

"Tom."

"Where are you from?"

"New Bedford, Massachusetts, the Whaling Capital of the World."

The staunch pride in this rehearsed answer made her chuckle. "So you've seen whales before?"

"In a museum."

Jane detected his loneliness and responded from the well of her own. Instead of the maternal instinct, that was what she had: this sensitivity to others' loneliness. In this boy she sensed such sorrow that she wanted him all to herself. When he brought a shark's tooth from his pocket to show her, she exclaimed. A cry went up about more porpoises sighted, but Jane and Tom ignored it. She saw her husband on the other side of the boat, talking to the woman with the babies. Then the diminutive man, whom she had noticed earlier with a dart of dislike, approached and clamped a hand on Tom's shoulder.

"Are you Tom's father?" Jane said, her gaze falling away from the man's hard stare. Behind dirty glasses, his eyes were a reptilian green. He didn't answer her.

To his son he said, "Are you seasick?"

"I don't get seasick," the boy said.

"You aren't even looking at these whales and stuff. What do you think we came up here for? So you could just run around on the boat?"

Though bareheaded, the man gave the impression of wearing a cap pulled low, and Jane shrank from him as she defended the boy: "He's telling me about New Bedford."

"Yeah, well, he talks too much."

Helplessly she watched as the father ordered his son below deck to bring him coffee. She glared at the man before turning her back on him. She wondered if this man used his fists on the child. Then she reassured herself, he cares about Tom enough to bring him on this unusual vacation. I shouldn't worry.

She found herself alone at the railing. It was a relief to turn away, to give in to what she thought of as her sickness. For she had been sick, and was recovering, hiding the cause from Kenneth and everybody else. In the past year, she had fallen in love, passion seizing her so completely that to remain in marriage now seemed unthinkable.

The man she loved was married too. He would never leave his wife. He was much older than Jane, and popular, in their town. Jane's best friend confided one day, in tears, that she was in love with him. As her friend unburdened herself of this great and dreadful secret, Jane sat stunned. Her sobbing friend couldn't speak his name aloud; she whispered it through swollen lips.

Suffering too, Jane told no one, thinking this could almost be funny if it weren't so awful.

She couldn't forget the day when she told him she loved him. He was the architect for a new wing on the school where she worked. For months he came by her classroom at the end of the day, while the shadows lengthened and Jane let her work go undone. He lounged against her desk, his long legs near her own as she sat in her wooden swivel chair, and they talked endlessly. Always he complimented her, in his low voice, and told jokes at which they laughed archly, her gaze clinging to his, and he reproved her wryly for her lancet remarks about her colleagues, then encouraged her for more. Jane went to work even when she had the flu, sustained by those late-afternoon conversations, hiding her fever. In the evenings she lay down morosely, so irritated by her husband's solicitude that she could have screamed.

The man she loved—Steven—had three daughters, all incorrigible. One was arrested for drug dealing. Another stole a neighbor's car. Why were they so bad? Jane wondered. She couldn't imagine that Steven was deficient as a father (he joked about starting a reform school out of his home), and she blamed his wife, a quiet lavender woman with the old-fashioned habit of gathering her skirt in her hand when she climbed a flight of stairs. They were in Jane's social circle. She knew few people her own age, twenty-nine. Generally she enjoyed knowing these older people.

She'd seen other women turn eager eyes on her husband's rock-hard face. People wondered why they had no children. Kenneth asked her when she planned to stop work. There's no need for you to work, he would say, we have plenty of money. But Jane had no intention of giving up her job, tiresome as it often was, for then there'd be no more afternoons of talk and laughter, time to store up every word he spoke to her, to replay when she went home. The late-afternoon sun was warm on the wooden floorboards of the classroom, warm on her face as she laughed up at Steven. He said it lit her hair like fire.

When the biologist left her seat to stand at the railing, Jane climbed up and took it. If the woman challenged her to regain the seat, Jane would say she didn't feel well. In truth, she felt fine. It was just her heart that always hurt, physically, as if bitten by sharks.

She found herself separated from the captain only by the round, old-fashioned compass and a tiller that he lazily steered with one hand. She smiled at him. "Tell me about this boat."

He was rawboned, with gray in his blond hair and his skin tanned hard. Behind his sunglasses he grinned at her as he told of traveling to British Columbia to pick out the tall trees from which he built the boat.

"With your own hands?" Jane said. Not educated, she thought, but smart.

He held out his hands, strong and blond-haired. He went south in winter, he said, to Florida and the Carolinas, and had no money, no savings or insurance, nothing except the schooner. He was married and divorced "a long time ago."

"So you're married to the sea," Jane said, and he liked that. He couldn't be the biologist's lover, she decided.

"There's one!" The cry went up from a woman in a flowered sun hat, standing just beneath Jane's high seat, pointing across the waves to the rising back of a whale the size of a city bus. Jane had the urge to swat the woman. Most people, she realized, she could watch get swallowed by a whale, Jonah-fashion, and not give a damn. She shaded her eyes and found Kenneth, still engrossed in conversation with the mother of three, and wondered what they could possibly have to talk about. The sight enraged her.

The captain said, "I wish I hadn't let that young mother bring her kids along. Their squalling is driving me crazy. Is that your husband with her? Where's *her* husband?"

"I wish they'd all fall overboard," Jane said. With pleasure she would toss the babies one by one, then shove the mother over, then Kenneth. Maybe then he would really look at her, for the first time in months.

"Don't cry," said the captain.

Jane hadn't realized there were tears on her cheeks.

"I used to go out with a girl like you," he said.

"I'm awful," she said. "I hate myself."

"You just think about yourself too much. Look at that lady in the flowered hat. Her mind's a dial tone."

Jane felt better. "What happened to your girlfriend, the one like me?"

"She died in a dance marathon."

"Right. And I'm a pirate."

"She really did."

"Are you and the biologist lovers?" Jane inclined her head in the direction of the large woman, now the center of attention of a knot of tourists gazing at a display of leaping dolphins. The fishes' backs shone in the sun, churning up a silver spray.

The captain's strong yellow teeth showed in a grin. "People ask me that all the time. On every single one of these whaling tours, somebody wants to know."

So which was it? Jane wondered, straining her eyes to see a distant fluke. He meant, Of course. No, he meant never. Yet if you lived on an island in the middle of a big bay, you'd be bound to bed down with some unlikely partners. You'd have so much quiet time to reflect, that you could figure out everything in your life, every single thing that had gone wrong.

"How far from land are we?" she asked the captain.

"A long way."

"What worries me," she said, "is that little boy with the mean-looking father," for the child was heading toward her again. "He's smarter than his dad, I can tell."

"Why worry," the captain said, spinning the tiller. He got out his cigarettes, put one between his lips, and went to fix a sail. Jane thought how his mind held a special vocabulary—boom, mast, mainsail. She thought how old-timey that was, and how pleasant.

"Tom, come sit by me," she said, and the boy scrambled up beside her. To her inquiries about his family, home, and school, he was monosyllabic, and Jane too fell silent and shy. The child's profile reminded her of a squirrel. She adjusted to their silence as she adjusted to the roll of the waves beneath the schooner. She watched her husband take a mug of coffee to the mother of three.

She thought about how last week she was so desperate for company that she let a proselytizer in the house. She had welcomed him in, looked at all his religious brochures, and served him cake. They talked about Hell. These last few months, she was feverish to make time pass, to put distance between herself and that terrible day when she said to Steven, "I love you," and he'd walked out of the room without a word, and since then had treated her with absolute cold professionalism.

During the time when their afternoon talks were at their height, she had even befriended his mother. The old woman lived across town, in a district once genteel, now dangerous; she was tight-lipped and sharp-spoken, a sewer inspector's widow. She boasted about her son, how brilliant he was, how fine looking; he wanted to move her to a new house but no, the one she had was good enough. One day she showed Jane a picture of him as a young man, saying slyly, "You can have it." Jane used the picture as a bookmark. The old woman derided her daughter-in-law. "He ought to have married somebody like you," she said, and Jane's heart lifted, thrilled. Tired of playing matchmaker, the old woman fell to criticizing her granddaughters. They would all get pregnant out of wedlock, she predicted, and be divorced three or four times. In the woman's wide mouth and high cheekbones, Jane saw something of Steven's face. But the pretext of her visits wore thin. One day the old woman fixed Jane with her syrupy yellow eyes and said, "Why do you come here?" and humiliated, Jane gathered her purse and jacket and crept out to her car. Yet if the old woman betrayed her to her Steven, he gave no sign of it. All he said was, "It's nice of you to visit her. Most people find her hard to take." Jane recalled the old woman's mothball-smelling house, a jar of laxative preparation on the stove, and she shuddered.

All this had reeled through Jane's mind as the prose-lytizer talked about hellfire. That's such a country music kind of word, Jane thought now as the Fundy wind rifled her hair—hellfire and teardrops. The prose-lytizer pressed more pamphlets into Jane's limp hands. His belly strained his polyester shirt. Go, she wanted to shout. Yet she had invited him in because she felt wild from her days of silence, when Kenneth was at his office and she was home alone with no sound but the heart-shaped leaves of the redbud tree tickling the windows.

He was the one who said good-bye first, thanking her for the cake and heading out the door. As he slewfooted his way down the hot street, she watched from the win-dow, thinking no one would ever love him madly, not in this human world.

To die in a dance marathon, she thought, gazing at the captain, now chatting with the biologist and the first mate. She wondered how he could trust the wind, how he knew that the tiller and compass, left to their own devices, wouldn't pull the ship helplessly to sea. To die in a dance marathon. Did the girl expire in a frenzy of stomping feet, her heels staccato on a wooden floor, her skirt whirling, arms triumphant above her head? Or did she sink slowly, head thrown back, a gathering weight in her partner's arms? Heart attack, what else could it be? You could have one even if you were young. High school boys, training for football in late summer, had heart attacks. You read about such things. What song was playing when she died? What steps did her dying feet try to follow? Why couldn't she just stop dancing, once she started to die?

She wondered if the captain had told the biologist about the marathon girl. She pictured the big woman lying awake at night, bedeviled by the dancing dead rival. Get to know anyone well enough, and you'd learn his worst pain. By that reasoning, no one knew her, for no one knew the depth of sorrow she felt.

Her best friend, sobbing, wracked with love for that man: she knew her best friend's pain, how it felt exactly. Jane was too far gone in her own torment to consider confessing it. She wondered if Steven simply had to have women in love with him, testing his desirability until a woman fell for him, until she said, "I love you." Jane had headaches all summer from thinking about it. Woodenly she offered solace to her friend, as they sat on Jane's screened porch, the bees heavy in the abelia bushes: "How long have you felt like this, how long have you known, does he know . . ." and after her friend departed, Jane cried. Why didn't he show up with two tickets for the Greyhound bus? She would go anywhere with him. The doorbell rang. She sat up and brushed the tears from her hot, stunned face, and went downstairs, but it was just the paperboy. She promised herself that she would ask Kenneth for a separation.

Having made this resolution, she was able to be cheerful with the paperboy, tip him nicely, and think about what to serve for supper. But she had said it before, and they had agreed to separate, and then they would do nothing; weeks and months would pass while they slipped further into their quiet rituals.

"There's a big one!" someone called, and the crowd turned its flagging attention toward a distant pair of flukes. Jane became aware again of the child at her side, so close their sleeves touched. Is your father good to you, she wanted to ask. She saw Kenneth, far down the deck, aim his camera. When the whale surfaced again, many cameras clicked, though the creature was so far away it would appear in their photographs as little more than grayness in the green water.

Wham! The boat lurched; people screamed; Jane clutched the railing.

"I saw what hit us," cried the boy, Tom, first to Jane, then to the crowd at large. "I saw it. It was big."

His runty father charged toward him. "Yeah? What'd it look like?"

"It was black."

"I don't believe you," said the father. "You're a liar." His voice was harsher than a slap.

Jane said, "Tom, tell me about it. I believe you saw it. We all felt it."

But the boy went to stand by himself at the rail, his hands behind his back in an adult gesture that tore at Jane's heart.

The captain turned the schooner around and they headed back. The wind was cold, and Jane headed to the backpack she had stored below, pulling out an extra sweatshirt. When she came back up on deck, two people spotted her and beckoned, and she stood irresolute—the young mother smiling, the captain waving, and Jane thought, This is my choice, my moment. She paused. Then she thought, It's not who I want to talk to, it's who I want to *be*. She chose the captain. They talked until the captain sailed into the safe harbor of the island, and the tourists, exclaiming over their sea legs, tottered off to find supper. They were delighted that the boat had been struck by a sea monster, and that they had survived.

"I'm a captain, don't you see?" Jane said to Kenneth in bed that night. She thought her heart would burst. She thought she sounded so petulant—after all Kenneth had done for her—yet she was trying to speak the truth. "You're a captain, too, and you need somebody like the woman with the three kids—not another captain. That's what's wrong with us. On the boat I knew this. Oh Kenneth, I'm so sorry."

Kenneth's silence was enormous in the darkness. "Fine," he said. He rolled onto his side, away from her.

Jane sat up and looked out the dark window. A mile down the island, on the other side of a cove, fireworks exploded in a tiny village called Castalia. She watched these fireworks, a modest and brief display, wondering what occasion they marked, just a celebration of summer? Was the biologist there with the captain? Jane longed to go somewhere with him. She lay down and tried to rest, for tomorrow she and Kenneth would leave the island.

She thought about Steven's improbable collection—all different kinds of barbed wire. He paid farmers to snip him lengths of it. At his house, during a party, Jane had admired the rusty twists, while Steven's lavender wife hovered behind them. He didn't know what to do with it, he said, smiling at Jane, so he just kept it.

Trying to sleep, all she could think about was how she hated him. Yet the more she hated, the more she loved. She pictured barbed wire buried in her skin; the more you tugged at it, the more you hurt yourself, as the backward spur dug your nerves and flesh. What she wanted from Steven was his whole life, she thought; she was even jealous of his dreams.

Beside her lay Kenneth, sleeping, Kenneth whom she had failed utterly.

———————

The next morning they boarded the ferry and sailed away from the island. It was a mild gray day, busy with transit. With the car stowed in the hold, Jane and Kenneth made themselves comfortable on the wooden seats of the passenger area. Smudged windows offered a panorama of Fundy Bay.

Then she spied the child, Tom, darting about on deck. She saw his squirrel profile. Feeling her gaze, he turned and waved, and Jane waved back. She had prepared for this. In her pocketbook she had a box of candy and a china mug with a whale on it, both bought at the inn's gift shop. She would give him these things with a hug. She would write down her address and ask him to send her a letter. But first, because she'd slept so little last night, she would take a nap. She lay down on the hard wooden bench. The ferryboat smelled of old popcorn. It rode the waves in long smooth glides.

She slept too long. Kenneth jostled her shoulder. Waking, she found that the ferryboat had docked, and she and Kenneth were the last on board. She sat up hastily, rubbing her eyes, and saw the little boy and his father already driving off the platform, driving away.

Merry-Go-Sorry

And I will cast abominable filth upon thee, and make thee vile, and will set thee as a gazingstock.
—NAHUM 3:6

IT BEGINS in an Arkansas courtroom: the trial of a young man for the deaths of three boys. It begins in late May, a year after the murders, on a day so hot that the air conditioning can't keep up with the sweat on the seventeen-year-old defendant's face. He has confessed, though his lawyer protests that the confession, taped in hysterical segments by the police and existing too in written form, signed in Sid's childlike scrawl, means nothing: Sid Treadway is mentally retarded, he says, and the police coerced him.

Sid Treadway's long scarred dumbfounded face follows his lawyer's striding figure to the bench and back, and then Sid's mild green eyes are distracted by a cicada thrumming on a courtroom windowsill. He recalls the last such insect he saw, at his sister's house, which died loudly, clatteringly, in a dish of lemons. He barely hears his lawyer. In revulsion, his sister had thrown out the lemons, which she had planned to use in a pie. She has not come to the courtroom; only Sid's father is there for him, Big Sid, who when his son was arrested had burst into sobs like a child. There will be another trial for Sid's alleged conspirators, one of them widely regarded by an outraged public as the ringleader. Sid's trial is separate because he confessed, implicating the other two.

Sid Treadway helped to slay three young boys and left them hog-tied, bleeding and drowning in a ditch, says the prosecutor.

That is what the jury believes, swiftly convicting Sid Treadway, but that is just the prelude, the beginning.

It begins again in the trial of Benedict James, the devil-worshiping, girlfriend-biting, trailer-dwelling dropout who had tutored his disciples Sid Treadway and Robert Abt in evil (so the prosecutor says, six weeks later in the same courtroom), who had targeted his three victims (their eight-year-old faces—one slyly mugging, another somber, a third, the most lovable, expansively smiling—have decorated Tennessee and Arkansas newspapers for months now). If the trial of Sid Treadway was easy, the trial of Benedict James and Robert Abt is as simple as calling Satan by his name.

In Benedict's closet there's nothing but black T-shirts and black pants, a police officer testifies, and his diary has poems he wrote to the devil.

Benedict's pregnant girlfriend, Victorine Stark, sits every day in the back row. Sixteen, red-haired, beautiful, she has pointed to teethmark-scars on her white neck for the benefit of photographers. She is carrying the child of the man she loves; this is her fate, she says. Her mother, thirty-two but looking sixty, sits beside her embroidering the face of Jesus on a pillowcase. Nobody loves *her,* she tells reporters, and she'll be grandmother to the devil, but she has a sweet lovely daughter, she says; I want the best for my girl.

Benedict of the shaggy black hair, the fishbelly-white skin, the deeply scalloped underlip, the pedophile's eyes, gets sent to hell right there in the Arkansas courtroom, as daily the trial ends with a curse: the father of one of the victims (who will himself be on trial within the year, for stealing furniture from a neighbor's moving van), rushes Benedict in a ritual that the guards and the jury have come to enjoy: Burn in hell, murderer! You killed my little boy! he cries. The guards let him get within arm's length of Benedict before gently tugging him out the door. Benedict sits unmoved, only his large stomach moving fast with his breath, his T-shirt lifting up and down.

The other defendant, Robert Abt, is vocal, whereas Benedict says nothing and does not take the stand. Robert Abt denies it all, the luring of the three young victims, the cutting, the binding, the rapes. But he gets confused. To the prosecuting attorney, he explodes, Damn you, man, you're trying to mess me up. His lawyer tells the judge that he has advised his client against taking the stand, but Robert Abt, age sixteen, insisted. I'm innocent, Robert Abt cries from the witness stand.

Benedict James is eighteen but looks older; he could be twenty-four or five. When the judge sentences him to death and asks if he has anything to say, he replies, No, sir.

Within six months, he's on television, complaining to an eager, rabbit-eyed interviewer about the regular rapes and the blandness of prison food. Yes, he says, he did bite his girlfriend during sex, just a lick, and he demonstrates with his tongue, while the reporter shudders. I don't worship Satan. I'm a white witch, a Wiccan, he says. I never said nowise else. He will not talk about the three murdered boys, whose faces flash again on the TV screen as Benedict is led handcuffed back to his cell on Death Row. Facing the camera, the reporter assures viewers that Benedict will be under lock and key until his execution; within minutes, the TV station is flooded with calls from viewers who express the wish that Benedict be raped every day for as long as he lives.

The drainage ditch, called Ten Mile Bayou, where the three young boys' bodies were found, still trickles through West Memphis past the truck stops and car washes. Now and then, somebody still leaves a wreath of flowers there; other such offerings, of wire and withered white silk, lie askew in the sludge, stuck in the ditchbank. Victorine Stark, in the trailer she shares with her mother, cuddles her newborn, a boy, and names it Malachi. That means "my messenger," she announces, with middle name Destiny. She had a vision, she tells a reporter who follows up on her story: on the day before the baby's birth, she saw a crow with a long strand of something in its beak, a long piece of videotape. It gave me hope, she says, her red hair spread out on the pillowcase with the Jesus face on it, while in the background, the baby whimpers and Victorine's mother spoons macaroni and cheese onto paper plates, inviting the reporter to stay for supper.

What do you think was on the videotape? the reporter asks indulgently. The one that the crow was carrying?

Victorine laughs, a sad gurgle that has caught on lately among the girls at her school, who copy the laugh and the way she wears her plentiful hair—loose with a tiny braid encircling the crown of her head. That videotape would be something pretty. It don't have nothing to do, really, with the crow. It would show the future my baby will have. Rising from her narrow bed, Victorine announces, I have memorized something from the Bible, from the Book of Malachi: *"Bring ye all the tithes into the storehouse, that there may be meat in mine house, and prove me now herewith, saith the Lord of hosts, if I will not open you the windows of heaven, and pour you out a blessing, that there shall not be room enough to receive it."*

The reporter, a young man whose instincts keep him at bay from this girl, but who has loved her violently since he stepped into her trailer twenty minutes earlier, saw her on the narrow bed, and heard the Arkansas honey in her voice, says, That's beautiful. I've never heard it before because I don't read the Bible.

Victorine holds his gaze with her green eyes, undoes her flouncy white blouse, and nurses the baby. It's getting dark outside; her mother hovers nearby to light candles that smell of patchouli oil. Victorine says, I still love Benedict, no matter what. Here's my favorite picture of him. She nudges the baby from her breast to draw something from the pocket of her blouse: a newsprint photo of Benedict bare-chested, his arms flung out in the shape of the cross. That was took just a few days before he was arrested, Victorine says. Sid Treadway took it. They was drinking and clowning around. You can have it. I've looked at it till it's in my heart forever. I tell my baby about his dad.

The reporter turns the picture over and discovers on the other side a coupon for a casino in Tunica: SEAFOOD BUFFET HALF PRICE. Victorine sees it too and says, I can't wait till I'm old enough to go play those slot machines.

The reporter tells her, I hope things turn out just fine for you. And you too, ma'am, he says to her mother.

You got me thinkin', Victorine says.

The reporter drives back to Memphis, over the bridge, with the scent of patchouli candles in his hair. For years afterward, while he entertains eligible young women in restaurants, he grows moody over his wine, imagines rescuing Victorine, taking her to the casinos that she dreams of. He tells himself she'll be old and fat by nineteen, but it is because of her that he does not marry until he is forty and the memory of her has faded to an outline of Arkansas trailer and nursing infant.

Oh, it begins, it begins a thousand times, as many times and ways as a heart can beat or break. It began when the victims were conceived, three boys—one of whom, Matthew, had he lived, would have committed sins at least equal to those he suffered; this secret was written in his genes and known only to God and to his mother, who had seen something that terrified her in his eyes one day when he came riding his bike out of the woods, April wind streaming across his fresh blond buzz cut, declaring, I'm the czar; beat a drum and blow a trumpet for me. Two weeks later, Matthew was dead. His mother assumed he had learned the word "czar" in school; that look in his eyes had matched the word, somehow. Glossing her lips in the years after the murders, after the trial, she looks in her mirror and thanks God that there is nothing of her dead son's gaze in her own face.

Yes I loved him, she tells herself, but not like I love the others. Her other children are twins, docile and calm, with a gift for mimicry. They go with her to pull weeds from their dead brother's grave, but doing so they talk about homework, church, cartoons. Both twins can do lots of cartoon voices, to the point where their mother goes weak with laughter, yanking pokeweed mechanically from Matthew's granite monument. The expensive stone bears in the center a porcelain photograph of Matthew, the somber one that ran for months in the newspapers. Matthew's mother was assured by the monument company that the porcelain picture will outlast even the monument itself. In five hundred years, a thousand years, Matthew's face will still gaze across the yard of the Presbyterian church.

We're as high as a cat's back, the owner of the monument company had said proudly as Matthew's mother picked out the stone and made a down payment, but we've been in business forever. Lady, monument companies come and go as fast as you can say tick, but we'll be here.

I didn't know the grave marker business had such a high turnover, Matthew's mother said, tearing from her checkbook a pastel check printed with a design of irises.

Yep, said the man, but not us. We been in business sixty years, and the last forty, the owner-manager's been me.

Because of the case, a newspaper photographer wins an award, having snapped a picture of the furious crowd outside the police station the day that Benedict James, Sid Treadway, and Robert Abt were arrested. The black-and-white image of those who gathered to see them brought into custody—the bared teeth, the lunging accusation, the scene electric with lynch-longing—finds a place in national news magazines and on the bulletin boards of thousands of newspapermen, amateur shutterbugs, and crime enthusiasts. In the picture, Sid and Robert hang their heads, their cuffed hands chafe at their backs. Benedict looks handsome in profile, his black hair tossed back from his high fore-head, his nose shaped like Elvis Presley's, but he's in handcuffs too, and he's hearing the jeers of the crowd that wants him torn apart.

The West Memphis police chief, Merle Neville, re-ceives the personal thanks of the Governor for cracking the case. Modestly he announces, I just listened to the buzz, meaning he has eyes and ears throughout the local subculture. I kept hearing Benedict James's name.

What of "Stonehenge," the abandoned cotton gin-house where Satanic rituals were long rumored to occur, Stonehenge, where word has it that Benedict used to sacrifice dogs, cats, rabbits, chickens? The farmer who owns it, burns the parts of it that will catch fire, and tears the rest of it down. It had sat so long on the edge of his cotton field, a high-roofed shed; not until after the arrests did it blossom with five-pointed stars and 666, and the farmer himself scratched its dirt floor for animal bones and found none, though he did dis-cover charred circles, which the police deemed ritualis-tic. (Aw, somebody roasted marshmallows out there, the farmer told police, while his wife said, Henry, that cult stuff is true; you just don't want to believe it. There were *orgies* going on out there. Do you think it was any-body we know?)

Merle Neville reassures the public, Your German shepherds are safe now. That's what those devil-worshipers want, is German shepherds.

The farmer resists even that; he does not know any-one who owns a German shepherd, he tells his wife.

Most everybody has hounds. The farmer owns a fat yellow Lab that lolls in the grass and snaps at flies as the farmer burns and dismantles his troublesome old cotton shed. To the dog he says, There were never any devil-worship meetings here. *You* know it and I know it.

Benedict James had played with a cat's skull, his classmates recall, jerking it up and down on a string in the second grade, when everybody else had yo-yos. He was seven, then; eleven years later he lured three little boys into the woods and with his two companions he sodomized and killed them, and then, according to Lyle Adair, a former friend of Benedict's who testified against him, Benedict bragged on it all. Victorine vouched that Benedict spent the night with her, but she could not account for the entire evening. She said it wasn't true that he wanted the baby named Lucifer.

He wanted me to give him a lullaby, but I wouldn't do it, Victorine had told the jury. He was with me right *after* them boys was killed. Don't get me wrong—he wouldn't do nothing so bad. But he wasn't with me at the time he said he was. So no lullaby.

She means alibi, her lawyer said.

There was another suspect, a man who had wandered into a Chicken Hooray restaurant the afternoon of the killings and covered the walls of the men's room in bloody handprints. The restaurant manager washed them off himself, disgusted, relieved when the man— wild, Indian-looking—went stumbling off without even ordering a meal. When the murders screamed into the news the next morning, the manager called the police and said, I saw the guy; he was here, all bloody. I knew something was wrong, but I didn't want to fool with him. I never saw him before nor since.

The restaurant sits on the highway close to the swampy field where the bodies were found. The investigators stopped by for fried chicken when the shifts changed and complained that the hot wings were too spicy and the chocolate malts too thin. That was when everybody thought some drifter had done it, a trucker or a hitchhiker stopping by to destroy kids who would have been out of school and into summer's liberty in just a few more weeks, kids who had played in the field and in the woods all their lives.

The restaurant manager weeps when Benedict, Sid, and Robert are convicted. To his wife and daughter, he says, They didn't do it. I saw the guy that did, but he's gone. I wish to God I'd left that blood on the walls. I wish I'd locked him in the men's room and called the cops. He did it, did it and got away with it.

The manager's wife says, Maybe he had just been in a fight. Those three creeps in jail, they're the ones did it.

Their daughter, Crystal, isn't listening. A wispy blonde fifteen-year-old with almost transparent skin, she is in love with Robert Abt, having fallen for him during the trial. She has even visited him in jail, secretly, making the trip by bus to the prison sixty miles away after telling her parents that she is at a friend's house, learning to sew.

Her father says, I will feel wrong for the rest of my life, like I'm wearing the wrong body.

His sobs sound wracking and unmanly to Crystal's distracted ears. She slips away to her room to write to Robert Abt, in a sacred ritual of pink stationery, calligraphic penmanship, and dabs of perfume on the envelope, always with a "LOVE" stamp, placed upside down. In school she had known Robert Abt vaguely; now she has pledged to herself that she will marry him, even if he stays in jail for the rest of their lives. Robert rarely answers her letters; she knows other girls love him too and that he could have his pick. Sid Treadway of the long pimply face and stigma of retardation and signed confession has no such following. Benedict James's admirers are the most varied, including the hardest-core of the tattooed high school girls, a number of quiet intellectual women who would never admit an attraction to him, and several stoned older women who alternately want to mother him and take him to bed.

The girls and the women, along with nearly everyone else in West Memphis, make donations to the reading grove that is established at the elementary school in honor of the murdered children: three sturdy benches donated by the local hardware store and a half-dozen oak saplings that will grow to shade the children of future years, who will linger there, the teachers hope, turning the pages of books, the oak leaves whispering above them.

Crystal, the daughter of the Chicken Hooray manager, gets A's in school without reading anything at all.

She pays attention in class. I don't read, but I can write, she tells her friends, meaning her letters to Robert, letters so hot and loving that even the recipient, stupid and angry in his cell, catches his breath as he holds the pink-mist stationery in his hands, the charm of passion searing his blood. He recalls her then. She has visited him three times: a blurry girl who weeps more than she talks, with blonde hair so thin her ears poke through it, reminding him of a lop-eared rabbit, yes he remembers her now.

To her friends, Crystal says mysteriously, Robert *knows something* about what happened, but he didn't do it. When her friends scowl, she sticks out her chin and says, He'd of told me if it was different.

What of the crushed roll of peppermints found at the crime scene, and the scrap of a handkerchief printed with a picture of a Hot Springs bathhouse? Why was one victim, David, missing his shoes, and where is the third bicycle, only two having been recovered at the scene? Who cared about mints or handkerchiefs when the bodies showed treatment that only the devil could have invented, or carried out?

One detective asked the chief, Why don't we arrest that Lyle Adair. We got as much on him as on the others. His name comes up just as often. He was seen at a laundry washing clothes with mud on 'em, and hauling a smelly secret box in the back of his car. Why don't we arrest Lyle Adair.

But Lyle goes free, a rangy, skulking presence who

skips out of West Memphis after the trial. The convicted ones are enough, and three is a magic number:
Sid Treadway, Robert Abt, Benedict James; three killers
for three victims.

Never mind that David would have grown up to be a
brilliant folklorist, that even at eight he knew that the
ballad "Barbara Allen" existed in at least ninety-two
forms, of which he could sing several, in a high clear
voice. Nobody knew where he got it, the curiosity about
the old songs or the beautiful voice. His mother, a hair
stylist, a tough gal who spends her Saturdays waxing her
jeep, says David just loved old songbooks. She doesn't
like those songs, she tells her friends; it used to bug her
when David sang about some Barbara Allen asking for a
grave long and narrow. He had a premonition, David's
mother says moodily, snipping little v's into a client's
bangs to give lift and volume, as the radio plays the
Statler Brothers. If I'd gone ahead and given him that
Game-Boy he wanted for his last birthday, he'd've put
those creepy old ballads out of his head. His dad and I
never sung 'em.

Not that she's with David's father anymore. Within
six months of the murder convictions, she has divorced
David's father. Matthew's parents were long divorced
already. The parents of the other victim, Troy, had
never married, though they had talked about it when
they were not involved with others. They had last dis-
cussed it—and decided against it—at a Halloween costume party the year before the murders, a party for
grown-ups and kids, he dressed as a crescent moon, she

as the sea, with Troy in tow as an undercover cop. It was a great Halloween party, Troy told his mother, his fingers deep in the sticky icing of a cupcake, amidst the flaring jack-o-lanterns and the flowing orange punch, though he had to keep explaining his costume to all the other kids: his old jeans and dirty T-shirt gave no clues. He had a squirtgun in his pocket, though, and a plastic badge on his chest, and late in the party he cut armholes in a paper sack and announced it was a bulletproof vest. His father, the moon, and his mother, the sea, got drunk enough on rum that they spent the night together, the crescent cardboard mask tossed on her bedroom floor, and her silver shawl, sequined in turquoise, catching the breeze from the window, that warm night. It is the crescent moon who rushes Benedict James in the courtroom some months later, daily during the trial, cursing him to hell and back until the final day when the judge sentences Benedict to death, until Benedict, when asked if he has anything to say, moves his scalloped underlip just enough to reply, No, sir.

The animal part of the legend grows: it wasn't just dogs and chickens sacrificed in McKenzie's cotton shed, the buzz goes, but horses and pigs, sheep and cows and babies of girls who were themselves raised by goats and bore on their foreheads the mark of Baphomet, the head of a goat inside a pentagram, young girls so far gone in depravity that they killed their own infants; they set the babies on a rock and raised the knife and you can still see the blood, the buzz said, look for the dark stain on the biggest rock on the floor of the cotton shed that McKenzie tore down. Babies' blood will never wash away, even if it rains forever.

McKenzie says to his wife, That triple murder was a sex crime. Didn't have nothing to do with the devil. That was just hype that the police and the lawyers thought up.

Satan works through men, through us humans, his wife says.

This is what Troy, the son of the moon and the sea, had done on the day he died. At school that day, he had been impressed by the science lesson: the teacher, a young man impassioned in his love for wildlife, had described a field experiment during a college biology class, during which time he had gone from nest to nest in a swamp, shaking the eggs of birds who had laid them there, birds that had invaded the nests of the rightful owners, rare endangered creatures of milder temperament. Troy pictured his teacher seizing the big speckled invaders' eggs and shaking them hard enough to kill the embryos inside. The teacher was kind, so Troy could not grasp the kindness in his shaking the eggs. It seemed so cruel to kill the baby birds inside.

After school, Troy found his friends Matthew and David. All three had bikes. With little conversation, they planned to race and play in the woods as they always did.

When the man at the woods' edge beckoned them to

follow him, Troy's mind was on those birds' eggs being shaken, even as he pedaled toward the forest with his friends. He felt sick at his stomach, thinking of his teacher shaking those eggs. Something tugged vaguely at his thoughts—*don't*—but his legs were churning and his bike sped into the darkness where the trees were and where the man waited.

Humble dreams, Sid Treadway's: to be a trucker in one of the rigs that whiz along I-40 and I-55, staying up all night to cover, oh, six, seven hundred miles. Even after months in jail, he has not realized, not really, that this will not happen for him, that he will never drive such a truck, unless as a very old man straining to read highway signs, his eyes too bleared for driving after dark. It's the driving that has always attracted him, not so much the places, not Chicago or San Francisco or St. Louis, just the fast hard nonstop travel that is sexual for him, the idea of it.

When a damning piece of evidence—a knife—was retrieved from a pond behind Sid's house, Sid's lawyer argued that it was old, rusty, and unidentifiable as the murder weapon. The jury eyeballed it, still sharp as a spearpoint, its handle wrapped with leather thongs, and decided this was it: Those killers thought they'd fooled us, flipping it into the pond when they were through cutting.

After the trial, Sid's lawyer fumed to his friends, There's knives at the bottom of every damn pond in the world, and they said, We don't think so.

Sid had been to Memphis many times. Just before the three little boys were murdered, he had visited the Pink Palace Museum with his father (Sid had long since dropped out of school, abandoning his special education classes) to see a display of elaborate mechanical dinosaurs. At first Sid thought they were real. Roaring giants, they reared back, then lurched toward him, their claws flexing, their great tails thumping the polished museum floor. His father, Big Sid, dared reach across the velvet rope and slap the haunch of a stegosaurus. The creature rolled its eyes at him, and father and son cried out, only the father was laughing.

They got some kinda sensor in there, Big Sid said. It ain't alive. Look at them feet. You can see gears and stuff that they tried to hide with rocks and a clump of fake grass.

I want to go home, Sid said.

Who else, then, was in the cult? Besides Benedict, Robert, and Sid, (speculation ran), a harelipped housewife comes under suspicion. She lives on the edge of town; she might slip out of her house to buy a quart of milk, and instead make her way to Stonehenge. Maybe McKenzie was in on it, people say, and his wife. After all, Stonehenge was on his land. Victorine of course was in the cult although who could blame her; Benedict had brainwashed her and would have eaten their baby had he not been caught in time. A dozen trailer-park teens, grunge-dressed, their ears dulled by endless playing of heavy metal CDs, tell tales of chanting and spells and wild sex, tales about each other and strangers too.

Thirty miles away, in another county, a man and a woman run a shop that sells roach clips, black candles, and wands. A cherry bomb crashes through their plate-glass window and explodes. The couple collect the insurance money and open a tanning salon. Business had been terrible, anyway, ever since the occult rumors got started about the killings. They were never devil-worshipers at all, the couple says; they are Methodists. Their tanning parlor, Sun Worshipers, offers discount coupons in conjunction with the pizza parlor next door. It's a hit.

Where were *you* that afternoon, that witching-hour of suppertime and twilight, that full-moon evening of sticky mild air and fierce mosquitoes, when the boys disappeared, leaving two of their bicycles mangled deep in the woods? Can you account for where you were every minute and with whom, and what you did and why? Suppose it wasn't Benedict or Sid or Robert or the bloody Indian-looking man in Chicken Hooray?

Suppose there's a man who knows the woods well; he's driven the service road to the highway a million times. He killed the little boys in a place near the highway, where the whizz-a-mizz sounds of traffic covered up their shrieks. By the time he read about the boys' disappearance, maybe he was rocking on his heels in Las Vegas. Through the newspapers, he followed the trial from Oregon, say, where he was backhauling trash to a landfill. He's on a fishing trip in the Everglades when he reads about the convictions. Every morning he buys coffee and newspapers from an old man at a little bait store. How 'bout them devil worshipers in Arkansas, the fisherman says, squirting milk into his Styrofoam coffee cup. The old man says, What about it. What is it you know. The old man has ears that could hear the splash of a body being rolled into a creek nine hundred miles to the northwest. He has God's eyes.

The fisherman grins into God's eyes and says, Fix me a egg sandwich, mister, and don't tell me you never wanted to bugger no little boy. He slaps Benedict's picture on the newspaper and says, This guy got fat during his trial, didden he? That's what happens when a vampire eats jail food. He was used to living off little boys' blood. He sucked blood from one of 'em's cock, old man.

He drives off in a car he stole in Georgia, a rusty alligator-green Crown Vic with a busted radio and bad shocks. When a hard morning storm catches him, he discovers the car leaks, rain splashing through the vinyl roof and onto his arm as he steers. No fishing that day. His stomach lurches, he has to pull over and roll out of the car into the brush to vomit. The egg sandwich, he thinks. He sees again the old man's eyes. His guts heave. He has heard of people dying from throwing up when they get snakebit. He thinks of that now as he convulses in the weeds, though he knows he wasn't bit. His money's almost gone. The rain stings the back of his

neck and slashes his bare arms, exposed in the cut-off
T-shirt. It feels like knives, but it's rain.

The moon's face is God's head turned backwards.
That's what a teen, brought in for questioning, told the
detectives as the investigation stalled, then picked up,
then gathered steam. Backwards, yes sir, the girl said,
identifying herself as a spirit sister of Victorine, picking
at her chipped black nail polish. Yes, she said, I had sex
with Benedict and Victorine both. We had went to a
carnival in Jonesboro and then we came back to Victorine's trailer and we was drinking. Later on I found
out Victorine was pregnant, the girl says, and I'm scared
she'll have Siamese twins because of what we done.
They're both so sexy, the girl said, Benedict and Victorine. I know I ought to care more about the three little boys that got killed, but the ones I love are Benedict
and Victorine and the baby inside her, please let it be
okay.
     She told the detective, I knew we was going to all
make love that night as we was heading to the fair. We
crossed this field that smelled all sweet like hay, and in
the distance I could see the ferris wheel lit up bright and
I heard the music from the fair, and I just knew. It made
me scared but so happy. I bet you didn't know anybody
could be as happy as I was.

There was a word that Benedict loved, his mother
says during the trial, speaking as if her son were already
dead. It was an old word, something he found in a

dictionary, a word that had not been used for centuries. The detectives write this word down: merry-go-sorry. It means a story with good news and bad, she says slowly, frowning, remembering. Joy and sorrow mixed together, yes, that's what my son used to say. He was always finding out old-timey stuff. Merry-go-sorry. Like if somebody had a lot of trouble in their life, but was still alive to tell about it. Ill fortune, Benedict used to say, and then something good happens to you. Good and bad smacking you in the face all the time. He's always been sad. He has not had much good in his life, but he's not an evil person. Just drugs and drink and getting that girl pregnant and no, he never killed no animals except maybe a bullfrog. He's on medication for sadness. I have tried. I have really tried. He seemed the happiest when we was living out in Washington state, a few years back, with his real dad. He went to school regular then and liked the snow and the mountains. Benedict James is the name he give hisself. When he was born, I named him Woodrow. His real daddy's last name is Gilson. He took his stepdad's name when he was twelve and searched through phone books looking for a first name. Benedict was the one he chose, so that's what he goes by and that's what them that loves him, calls him.

Luminol: what a beautiful word. It makes blood glow in the dark, the egg-shaking science teacher tells the class. Policemen use it to find where people were killed. They used it last year when your friends Troy, David, and Matthew were murdered. Luminol has to be used at night. The police are our friends. They went into the woods at night and sprayed the Luminol on the ground around the ditch where the boys were found, and it lit up like sunset. Phosphorescence: here let me write it on the board, but I've never been any good at spelling. Y'all are better spellers than I am. Everything leaves a trail. Do you pray for your friends who died? Let's all bow our heads right now.

Crystal, in love with Robert Abt and writing him every night now in the privacy of her own room, a room bedecked with angel suncatchers, bowls of potpourri, and posters of handsome TV stars bare-chested in leather jackets, knows that sooner or later her mother will find out about the correspondence. Propped up on pillows on her pretty bed, she expects her mother to barge in, knock the clipboard and the pink-mist stationery off the bed, and seize her by the ear, declaring, Don't you *fool* with that killer, you hear me?

Yet weeks pass, and Crystal mails the letters each morning in secret at the mailbox near her high school. Growing bolder, she displays a picture of Robert Abt that she clipped from a yearbook. She sticks the picture in the frame of her mirror so she can look at his defiant face while she brushes her thin blonde hair. In dim light, his eyes follow her movements as she tosses her head, brushing her hair as if it's tresses, a word she doesn't know how she knows.

One night her mother enters the room with a basket

of fresh clothes, spots the picture, and says, Who is this? Crystal puts down her pen and says, It's who I love.

Setting the laundry basket at the foot of Crystal's bed, her mother goes to the mirror, plucks the picture from the frame, and holds it up to the light. He's one of them three, she says, but with more caution than censure. Crystal waits for outrage, but her mother turns the picture this way and that, then chuckles. He could be in the church choir. Look at that stripe tie and that pressed shirt, she says.

I write to him every day, Crystal says, and sometimes I go visit him. I'm almost grown. Don't try to stop me.

How can anybody stop their kid from growing up? her mother says, laying the picture gently on Crystal's dresser. It's just 'cause he's in jail, and will be until he dies, that he seems like anything at all to you. You write to him all you want, but don't expect me to sew you any white gown for a jailbird wedding, if it gets that far. I bet he's got *sacks* of letters from girls.

Are you mad, Mama? Crystal asks, confused not by her mother's words—they're nearly what she expected—but by her tone, curiosity mixed with scorn and sadness.

Your daddy thinks that Indian-looking guy did it, the one came stumbling into Chicken Hooray, but I think the police got the right ones. Those three jerks in jail did it. The jury decided it and the judge just knew. If your Romeo got out tomorrow, he wouldn't seem so hot. Here's your bras and jeans I washed for you. Oh honey,

Robert Abt can't take you to the prom. Find somebody who can.

I'm not going to any prom, Crystal says, glorying in the sacrifice of it all—turning down boys who would ask her. If she chose to, she could spend all afternoon with her hair in curlers, putting on her makeup, pulling on a tight dress with rhinestones on the straps, but she won't. She will take the bus to Cummins prison on that fine spring day and get home late, smelling the apple blossoms in the air and hearing the distant music over at a rented dance hall. Already there is talk among the juniors and seniors of holding the prom at the Holiday Inn, a place of such sophistication that Crystal's heart nearly bursts with longing to go there, but no, she tells herself, I will not.

Suit yourself, honey, her mother says. Proms is too expensive these days anyhow. Kids think they have to rent limos, for God's sake. Your daddy and I had one of them old-fashioned proms with crepe paper streamers strung up in the gym, and it was just as good that way.

Did y'all drink back then? Did you go all the way? Crystal sits up straight on her bed. She has never dared to ask her mother these things.

Of course we did. We still do, and I bet that shocks you more. Her mother laughs and leaves the room.

Crystal sits on her bed, the writing paper scattered across her lap, remembering something: the way her grandmother used to address her mother, Crystal's mother. She used to call her Daughter. Crystal's gaze falls on Robert's picture and it's her grandmother's voice she hears, saying, Daughter, I won't see you as a murderer's bride.

She picks up her pen again and writes to him. The memory of her dead grandmother has awakened something in her, a whole chain of memories. She writes them down for Robert: do you remember, she asks him, as if they are seventy-five instead of fifteen and sixteen. Do you remember the way our elementary school used to play chimes before the principal spoke over the intercom. We'd hear a xylophone and then Mr. Butsavage would speak. Isn't that a funny name. I never heard a funnier one.

Crystal writes many other memories in her letter, but that's the only one that Robert Abt reads. He remembers Mr. Butsavage too, and he hurls the letter to the floor of his cell with an oath. He still remembers a beating the guy gave him, the old wooden-paddle kind. But he can't remember why.

There was a boy in an Arkansas town who wore a long black coat even in summertime, who walked along the levee speaking in verse, waving his hands with their long fingernails at the sky, squinting at the sun. The prettiest thing he'd ever seen, he told his friends, was a little girl with long blonde hair down at Gulf Breeze, Florida. He'd been there long ago. Her hair was so yellow and the sea so green. The sky was green too, because it was about to rain, and Benedict liked rain.

He used to gesture across the river at Memphis and

mention a famous movie star who lived there. He'd tell his friends, I know friends of *hers.* They say she's the person they used to go to back in high school when they wanted somebody beat up. She'd get somebody to do it, or she'd beat 'em up herself. Benedict would make his group of followers pause and stare across the river, through the haze that hung always above it, at a pale smudge of townhouses on the cliffs: see that white house on the bluffs? That's hers.

How do you know these people, these friends of hers, a doubter asked. I think you make stuff up.

Maybe I do, Benedict said, and maybe people tell me stuff. Secrets. I like to think about that movie star beating people up in high school. I'd like to take her on.

She's old, man, somebody said.

But she's pretty, said Benedict. One time I was with a lady who was fifty years old, and she was damn sexy. You got no idea, he said to his friends.

So he loved the memory of the little blonde girl by the green Gulf. He loved the river, with its floods and the slow barges moving their cargoes of coal and timber from St. Paul to New Orleans. He loved the long flat Arkansas roads with cotton fields on either side, and mud puddles, and the painted wooden fake windows, nailed to the sides of small white churches, that serve as stained-glass "windows" for Arkansas congregations that don't have any money.

His own church was his room, where he wrote in his journal and burned his candles and loved and tormented his girlfriend, Victorine, on a bare mattress.

The rest is all legend, what they say he did with animals and with those little boys.

Isn't it.

Another baby is growing inside Victorine's belly, this time a black man's child. She took a black man for a lover as easily as she might help herself to a slice of pie. Of all her lovers, and even at sixteen and a half she already has trouble keeping count of them, this man is the one she loves the most, the one who makes her forget about Benedict (whom she had loved despite—because of?—the neck-biting, the two-timing).

This man is a groundskeeper for an old cemetery in Memphis. She met him at a quick-mart where he was buying gas for his truck. He looked at her as she passed by him, a hungry look that held in it a dream, not just of sex but of something lasting. She waited in the store, resting the baby, Malachi Destiny, half on her hip, half on the frozen foods case. She had come to buy herself a Fudgsicle, but now in her mind there was only waiting. The man came in the store and paid for the gasoline and then came straight to her with his deep eyes, hungry and waiting, too.

He said, I noticed you came here on foot. Would you like a ride, you and the little baby.

Victorine opened the ice cream case, which steamed frozenly up into her face. She reached in and plucked out a cup of strawberry ice cream. The man stood beside her, all quietness, older she saw when she looked at him again, older than she'd thought at first, yet with energy and newness.

I'm tired, she told him. I'm tired of everything. I live in a trailer with my mother, and I have this little boy. We don't have a car.

What's your name, he asked her, and she told him.

I'm Zebulon, he said. He took the cup of ice cream from her hand and bought it for her, then held the door as she went outside into the beautiful day (it was February by then, and warm the way the Delta can be in late winter, with the trees already wreathed in palest green). The trials had been over for a few weeks, and the baby was fussy, wearing Victorine out in the trailer all day. Benedict, when she visited him in jail, did not care about anything, he said. Zebulon held the door of his truck open and Victorine climbed into the passenger side. The truck was neat and clean and smelled like the man. She thought about how Benedict would have made her buy the ice cream herself and buy some for him, too. When Zebulon got behind the steering wheel and started the truck, she turned to him and said, Make me laugh. I haven't laughed in a long time.

He held the baby while she ate her ice cream.

That very afternoon he took her to Elmwood, the cemetery where he worked. She had not known there were whole cities of the dead, with lanes marked like city streets and communities of sorts laid out: for the yellow fever victims, for the Memphis Jews and Memphis Chinese, for the Woodmen of the World (some old-fashioned self-help group, Zebulon said), and row after row of Confederate soldiers. Huge trees stretched out their massed limbs above the graves, so that the whole place was a garden, and the ground was hilly like the old Indian mounds that Victorine used to play on as a child. Eighty acres, but it feels like a thousand, said Zebulon, proud. He said: One evening I saw four men all dressed in white, at the tomb of that there Napoleon Hill (with a jerk of his chin he indicated a cotton factor's grave), and they were disappearing.

What do you mean? asked Victorine.

Fading away. And I saw a little child one time, sitting on that stone there, the one with an upside-down torch, meaning a life untimely ended, extinguished you might say.

I want to be buried here, Victorine said. Is there room?

Yes, but it's high, said Zebulon. He showed her a new grave and said, Just the marble itself cost a hundred thousand dollars.

The air grew darker and colder as they wandered, the baby asleep in Victorine's arms. She could hear the highway distantly on one side of the cemetery and a slow train moving behind the trees, but all around were just the silent graves.

Here's a man who went drinking on Front Street a hundred years ago and was never seen again, said Zebulon. Jasper Smith his name was. See the stone bale of cotton beside him. And here's two stone feet underneath a stone tree trunk—that's a lumberjack killed in

Arkansas when a tree fell on him. His ma even had his feet measured so the stone feet could be made the right size.

But the stone that Victorine fell in love with was an angel, pointing to heaven with her fingers worn off by rain and time. She had a diadem in her hair, a diadem topped by a star. Victorine fell to her knees on the damp winter earth and wept. Zebulon knelt beside her and said, I have a wife and two daughters. I have always kept my marriage vows, but now I want to spend time with you.

That much felt familiar: Benedict had not been true to her either; she had not been his only girl. Victorine raised her eyes to the angel. Who is buried here, she said.

A slave dealer killed in a duel, he said. Here now, he said, don't wipe your eyes with that handfulla grass. Take my handkerchief.

The handkerchief was fresh and white, pressed as for church. He didn't touch her that day. That came later, and when it did, so lovely, even in her passion she remembered the angel, the clean handkerchief, the strawberry taste of ice cream on her tongue.

Where are they buried, the three little boys? None in the old cemetery in Memphis where Victorine's new lover mows the grass and listens to the silence and to the trains and the cars passing fast on the highway behind a screen of trees. One is buried in Alabama, where his mother's people are: that is Troy, whose mother costumed herself as the sea. The cemetery is new, with the stones flat to the ground. Little David lies in Chicago, because his grandparents on his father's side pitched a fit lest he be laid to rest in the town where he was killed. Only Matthew was buried in Arkansas, Matthew who had he lived would have killed someone, too, and maybe many. His mother, who with her twins pulls weeds from his stone, wonders at how the weeds got a foothold so fast in the soil. She still hears the church bells ringing all over town as they did on the day of his funeral. Fine, she thinks, trying to end it. This is what was meant for him. I told him not to go into the woods. I told him.

You can drive the back roads of Arkansas for a hundred years, past Indian mounds, past swamps where turtles cling to logs and slip underwater when your car rumbles by. You can pass through towns so small they have no sidewalks, where the autumn leaves scuttle through unpaved streets; inside the old shotgun houses that used to be sharecroppers' cabins, people love and fight and worry about money and children. Getting on toward dusk, you pass a barred owl perched on a sign, a black-striped sign that indicates a small bridge over a creek. The owl's broad face swivels around to follow your car, its gaze so fierce you back up to look at it again: it doesn't scare. It will hunt into twilight, hunt the mice in the grass and the flocks of blackbirds that whirl like a spray of pepper above fields of cotton and beans.

All over the Mid-South, an ice storm strikes in the winter after the trials, a storm so brilliant and terrible that power is out for weeks in parts of Arkansas, western Tennessee, and northern Mississippi. What's beautiful happens by accident: at the Memphis Fairgrounds, used as a gathering site for toppled trees and piles of brush, tons of debris ignite spontaneously into a colossal, magnificent fire, visible even across the river in West Memphis, where people jump up from their supper tables to stare, glorying and fearing, for it puts them in mind of Judgment Day.

Merry-go-sorry: a word that Benedict wrote in his journal and taught to his mother, a word detectives pointed out as Satanic, though Benedict had merely looked up the phrase in the Oxford English Dictionary.

It begins with three boys alive, then dead, it begins when they were conceived, when the man or men who bound them and knifed them were boys themselves. It never ends, not with Crystal setting down her pen and dreaming of Robert Abt in jail, or with Victorine nursing her two babies, both biggity—that Arkansas word that just means big—a pale biggity son and a dark daughter ("Amaziah," she named the girl, untroubled by the fact that Amaziah in the Book of Chronicles was a king who set up false gods and was ruined; she just loves the name)—Victorine with the two babies at her breasts, happy enough with her children, or with Farmer McKenzie gazing up into the high ceiling of his barn where a hayfork hangs suspended, its spiked jaws chilling him: one frayed spot in the rope and the rusty fork could fall. He wants to believe some phantom killed those kids, not three young men possessed by Satan, as so many of his neighbors say, or three young men not possessed.

From his farm it's not far to the woods where Ten Mile Bayou spills its dirty water through the forest and out into the fields. Sowing and reaping, he adds up what he knows and finds it wanting.

Mayflies

IT WAS supposed to be Tyler's insect collection, but his mother kept finding the bugs. "There's a great biggie down at the end of the driveway, Ty," she'd say, or, "I just swatted one on the windowsill of the guest room," or, "Something with long antennas crawled out of the drain, go look." Most of his specimens therefore were already smashed and desiccated. He felt like an undertaker. Their deaths had no preparation or fanfare, and it disturbed him that a cicada could just die at the end of the driveway, or a honeybee expire on a pantry shelf.

"It's a sad project, a sorrowful time," he said to himself, and his mother, overhearing, told her friends what he had said and tried to make him repeat it.

"Don't you see how funny it is?" she said.

He didn't. The insect collection weighed on him, the guilt and horror of it. Weeks after he had impaled a wasp on a pin, he saw it move its wing. So his mother's nail polish remover killed them that slowly, its fumes were but a drug, the cotton balls soaked in Cutex at the bottom of his killing jar were mere chloroform. He was torturing living creatures.

It was August. The long snore of thunderstorms made it hard to sleep at night. In the mornings, he lurched fearfully awake, thinking at first that he heard his mother having a fit. But she was only laughing. She called it the cure. Ever since Tyler's father had left, back in June, his mother had vowed to have a belly laugh every day as a way of warding off depression.

"It's good for your whole body," she informed Tyler. "The positive effects are not yet understood."

He didn't argue with her. When she asked him to bring home joke books from the library, he obeyed. Still, it was startling to wake to the wheezing of mirth in the next room. He realized he had never laughed early in the morning. He didn't ask her what she thought about.

Something else was new, too: his mother's job. She'd found employment at a cheese shop. The good part was that she brought home samples of wonderful cheeses. Up to now Tyler hadn't realized there was anything except Swiss and American. He found he liked Brie, Camembert, Stilton, chèvre. The bad part was, he felt sure that everybody in town could make their own belly laugh cures out of his mother. She had taken to wrapping her head with cheesecloth, yard after yard of it, until her head was a big thick white turban. The cheese nun, he thought. No hair showed, just her broad cheeks with the cheesecloth bulging out on the sides, at the top, and in the back of her head.

"Why do you do that?" he said, as she stood before her mirror in the morning.

"To be professional. You'll notice I also wear this clean white uniform."

"Nobody else in that shop wears cheesecloth on their head."

"In France they do. I saw a picture in a magazine. I'm ambitious, Tyler. If you want to get somewhere, you have to dress for the top."

He told himself maybe it was just a good way to keep hair from getting into the cheese. Still he was ashamed and repulsed. The worst part was when she drove him someplace. Resolutely he wouldn't look at her beside him in the car. Her huge turban cast strange shadows in the sun.

Soon school would start, but for now, the pattern of their days was haphazard. She went to work and he went to the swimming pool or just stayed home working on a radio kit his father had given him. The bug collection preyed on his mind. It would be due in his seventh-grade science class in September. Out in the fields he saw his classmates with butterfly nets, and he felt sick. In the evenings his mother came home, fixed supper with a dessert of cheese (apparently another thing they did in France) and then they watched TV together, shows about religious cults that killed people, kidnap victims enslaved by motorcycle gangs, and most disturbing of all, criminals who escaped back into society and were living among regular people. "He goes by the name of Al and has a tattoo of a tiger on his chest," the announcer would say of a serial murderer. Tyler's mother enjoyed the shows, her eyes on the screen as her fingers expertly shaved slivers of cheese from a cutting board on her lap. Haunted, Tyler scanned the daytime swimming pool crowd for tiger tattoos.

Sometimes his mother came home with a crazy look in her eye, made him get in the car and go out to his father's new place. His father was an anchorman for a Richmond TV station. He'd rented a little farm out near Laurel and named it "Sweet Haven," the name of Popeye's house, or boat, or something. And his father had a horse, which seemed to anger his mother even more than the fact that his father had a girlfriend. His mother would park the car across the road and just stare up at the house. Its long driveway had a curve in it, whereas Tyler's driveway was long and straight. The houses were similar: white clapboard farmhouses that looked ever more out of place in the suburbs, with tall old trees shading them. The horse lived in a big field in front of the house, with barbed wire separating the field from the road. Once they saw his father's girlfriend come out of the house and whistle, and the white horse grazing in his field whinnied and cantered up to meet her. It was a beautiful sight. Tyler replayed it over and over in his mind as he and his mother drove home. In silence, they watched a TV show about severe constipation. Tyler lay awake that night picturing his father's girlfriend and the horse running up to meet her. The next morning his mother's laughter sounded like she was throwing up.

One day a new kid moved into the neighborhood, technically next door, but a quarter-mile down the road from Tyler, with straggly woods in between. Riding his bike down the road, Tyler saw the truck with boxes on it and the mother and father unloading things with their hair all wild and their faces worn out. He pulled the bike up into the driveway. This house was as old as Tyler's house, but weaker looking and needing paint.

Then he saw the kid. He was under a big elm, dealing cards in front of his crossed legs. Sometimes he yelped and smacked the cards. He looked up as he heard Tyler's tires. Tyler went nearer and stood over him.

"Ain't no fun playing slapjack by yourself," the boy said. He flipped another card on the pile and slapped it.

"That's a baby game," said Tyler, leaning his bike against the elm. The new boy had a bullet-shaped head and slanted green eyes and an out-of-town haircut. Tyler had an urge to scare him. "Tell you what, if you're in the seventh grade, you oughta be worried. You've got a bug collection due the first week of school."

The boy said, "The hell I do. When you're new, you ain't responsible for stuff like that."

Tyler held his ground, staring down at the boy. "Everybody has to do it. You better get some flies together."

"I wouldn't fool with no flies. I'd catch me some nice fat spiders and a bumblebee."

"Spiders don't count. They're not really bugs."

The new boy burst out laughing. He eased back with his legs crossed, as if his hip joints were rubber. His slanted eyes were slits. His feet kicked at the pile of cards.

"Massey, you come over here," the boy's mother yelled. She was holding a TV set in her arms as if it were a baby. "You help us now." She took the TV set into the house and came back out again and said, "Put them cards away!"

The new boy ignored his mother. He took his time sitting up, letting his laughter sink to a dribble. Dirt and leaves clung to his T-shirt. He shook his head. "What kind of a dummy school you go to, to say a spider ain't a bug? I'll tell you something. Today I seen Spider-woman herself."

"What do you mean?" Tyler said.

"A woman with a egg sac on her head. Great big egg sac like a spider makes." He arched his hands around his head.

"Massey, you get up here, boy!" This time it was the father who yelled. He lifted a bushel basket full of clothes. A cat jumped out of the basket and ran into the trees. "You can't just lay around all day."

"Where? Where'd you see this woman?" Tyler said.

With a grin, Massey wrinkled his nose. "At a cheese place. I won't never go back there no more. I don't want no spiders messin' with any of *my* cheese. I reckon I could put that lady in my science project—

World's Biggest Spi—Spi—" Once again he dissolved in laughter.

Tyler reached down and punched him in the nose. Easily as an acrobat, the new boy raised his feet and kicked Tyler in the stomach. Gasping, Tyler staggered backward. Massey was still laughing. Tyler was incredulous and enraged.

"Is she your girlfriend?" Massey drawled. "That cheese lady?"

"Don't you ever, ever say anything about her again," Tyler said. He got back on his bike.

Massey chuckled. He gathered his cards and shuffled them.

"Massey, this is the last time before I whup you," the boy's father called.

"Go swat me a fly, smarty pants," Massey instructed Tyler. He stood up. "I got work to do."

"I've warned you," Tyler said. He rode off hating Massey. Whatever had hurt him in his other life, whatever had filled his slanted green eyes with tears or packed his skinny chest with sadness, why, those bad times were just over for that Massey.

Bonnie, his father's girlfriend, was the weather girl on the TV station that his father anchored. Tyler's mother had dubbed Bonnie "Miss Heat Lightning." She'd ask, "Is Miss Heat Lightning calling for rain?"

After his visit with Massey, Tyler went home and turned on the TV set. There was Bonnie, giving her noon report. The camera ran up close so that her face filled the whole screen. She had on a stretchy orange tube top. Her lipstick looked like soft gold metal. She was laughing.

"It's gonna stay hot," she cried, pointing at a map, showing a warm front sweeping down from the Blue Ridge. "See? This low-pressure zone's sitting right on us. Yes, tonight it'll be sheet-kicking weather!"

Abruptly the camera switched back to Tyler's father, who looked amused as he gave the news. Anybody could tell there was something going on between them, Tyler thought. They looked silly.

When his mother got home from work, she pulled off her cheesecloth turban and announced, "Miss Heat Lightning was fired! Did you see that noon report? About the sheet-kicking? Well, the station manager said she'd gone too far that time. Too frisky for her own good. I called up your father to find out. Oh, he defended Miss Heat Lightning. He went into the manager's office and threw a royal fit. But Miss Heat Lightning is history!"

"Then Dad'll come home," Tyler predicted.

"What makes you say that?"

"She'll be crying. He doesn't like a lot of fuss."

"It won't make any difference if he tries to come back. We're through. Here, have some smoked Gouda. So good it'd make a bulldog break his chain." She put a piece in her mouth and chewed richly. "This was a happy day," she said.

Tyler's father did come over, the very next day. Tyler had gone out looking for bugs and when he got back, at suppertime, his parents were in the kitchen. His father sat very straight at the table, moving his shoulders to give emphasis to his words, the way he did on camera.

"I never cared a thing about Bonnie," he said, moving his shoulders on the word *thing*. "She's too young for me. I've seen the light." He raised his chin on *light*. "Every night she wants to go dancing down at Shockoe Slip. I'm sick of that. Take me back, Sherry." He smiled at Tyler's mother. "Are you bald under that thing you wear?"

"You can't come back. Under the terms of our legal separation, that would be illegal."

"Bonnie's gone back to her old job as a waitress. You don't think I'd go around with a waitress, do you? No, I want me a fine prestigious cheesewoman!" He saw Tyler. "Hey buddy, give me a hug." His whiskers scratched Tyler's cheek. "I found a nice big spider for you at home, behind the toilet. Want to come get him?"

"Spiders aren't bugs, Dad. Everybody just thinks they are."

"Sure they are. I studied science too."

"They've got eight legs. Bugs have only six."

His father laughed. To Tyler's mother he said, "Can I at least have a cheese sandwich?"

"You left me for Miss Heat Lightning," Tyler's mother said. "Now Miss Heat Lightning's in her hour of need, and you decide it's time for a cheese sandwich. But really, your doings have little to do with mine now. I've fallen in love."

"What?" said Tyler and his father.

"Yes," said Tyler's mother. "With a man who came in the cheese store. Unfortunately, he has a wife and son. But the attraction was instant, at least on my side. They're new in town. I asked him, What do you do for a living? and he said he's a paperhanger. I said, Have you ever done it with just one arm? and he said, Done what? and I said, Hang paper, like in the joke—busier than a one-armed paperhanger. I asked him, What did you think I meant?"

"Don't give him a chance," said Tyler's father.

"I should have asked him where they live," said Tyler's mother. "But it wouldn't matter. I don't intend to complicate his life. I'll just enjoy the feeling of being in love. So what if he has bad grammar? He says *ain't,* which I think is sexy. He's the kind of man I'd like to go joyriding with, ride out in the country and buy a ham and a gun and fireworks."

Tyler's father stood up and stretched. "Sounds more fun than my plans for the evening. I'm going to fill in my groundhog holes so my horse won't step in them and break his leg." He grinned at Tyler, then went outside and drove away.

The next morning Tyler woke up with the wish to see Susan Brown. She was a girl in his class who kept rabbits. He liked the quiet way she had with her rabbits. He liked her short hair and her habit of figuring things out. She got all A's.

He walked to her house, not far away. There she was, out in her yard tending her hutch. She had a big silky black rabbit in her arms. Its green eyes rolled up at Tyler.

"I thought they all had pink eyes," he said.

"Just the white ones," said Susan. "This one's my favorite. I know I shouldn't play favorites, but I do."

"Can we race them?"

"Okay." She handed him her favorite and lifted another one, a brown one, from the hutch. They placed them on the ground, side by side, and marked a finish line with twigs. "On your mark, get set," said Susan.

"Go," said Tyler.

The rabbits stayed where they were, chewing grass.

Susan said, "They're smarter than they might seem. Do you remember Muffin, my first one? She could turn on the water faucet." There was a pause. "Muffin died."

Susan put the rabbits back in the hutch. Tyler watched her neck bend as she leaned over.

"I cried about her for a long time," she said. "Sometimes I still do."

"I can't stand losing things," said Tyler.

"I think we can get so things don't hurt us as much," Susan said. "You can take shortcuts with feelings, just like with math problems or mysteries. I can figure out a *Nancy Drew* mystery story before Nancy Drew does. But feelings are harder."

"How's your bug collection coming along?"

"I hate doing it," Susan said.

"I'm not going to do one," Tyler announced, amazing himself.

Susan flung her arms around his neck and kissed his cheek. "Then I'm not going to, either. Getting a zero will be better than killing butterflies."

"Bye," he said. He walked down the road from her house, then turned and went back. She had gathered several cicada shells and was admiring them stuck to her palm.

"I think about you, Susan," he said. "I like to look at you. A person can be themself around you."

He smiled at her, and she smiled back.

Too curious to stay away, he went to see Massey again.

"It's my birthday," Massey said through the screen door. "Want some cake?"

The cake had black icing, which Massey said he'd asked for. He and Tyler ate the corners off the cake. His father was off hanging paper, Massey said, and his mother was at the grocery store.

"Last night we had artichokes," Massey said in disgust. "Artichokes, fartichokes. Them little shingles stick in your teeth."

"I'd eat 'em," said Tyler, feeling lofty. "I eat anything."

"Bet you ain't never eaten wart medicine. Compound W. I have. It's right good."

"I've gotten high. Off the air in a freezer chest," said Tyler.

Massey's green eyes looked canny. "My dad shares his joints with me. I've seen my old man broke and I've seen him broker, but he can always afford that stuff."

The kitchen smelled of peaches. Tyler looked around. He could tell the family was poor. An old-fashioned wringer stood in the corner. The tablecloth beneath their plates had holes in it.

"This is a turned-around kind of week," Massey said, leaning back in his chair. "My old lady went to buy fancy fixin's cause they're gettin' married today."

"Married!"

Massey laughed. "I been teasin' 'em 'bout being common law. They been together fourteen years without that piece of paper and now they're gunna make it legal."

Tyler put his fork down. He smiled.

"What's so funny?" Massey said. "Hell, it is funny." He chewed his cake. "I seen a cute chick playing with rabbits. I'm gunna go see her. I'm gunna think about her while I shave."

"Leave her alone," said Tyler.

Massey hooted. "You aimin' to protect all the women in town from ol' Massey? The cheese lady and the rabbit girl?"

"The cheese lady's my mother."

Massey laughed so hard he slid right out of his chair. Black icing made a mustache on the sides of his mouth. "That lady's so pent-up about something she's about to bust. I'd like to see it when it happens."

"She's happy. She's in love."

"Well, great, man! Everybody's *got* to be in love!" and Massey fell to laughing again.

Tyler's mother was putting a piece of iron under the hydrangea bush, to make it turn bluer, and Tyler was helping her dig under the bush, when his father showed up with a split lip.

"That's what I like about you, Sherry," said Tyler's father, flicking dried blood from his chin. "You care about how blue a flower is."

"What happened to you, Dad?" Tyler asked.

"Oh, I beat up a paperhanger," said his father, "and it wasn't even the right one. There was a guy hanging paper at the TV station, and I went up to him and said, Are you new in town? and he said Yep, so I socked him. And he socked me. Then I thought to ask him about the cheese shop, and he said, I don't know any cheese shop, and I said, Buddy, have a drink on me. I gave him some folding money."

"Does it hurt?" asked Tyler. The red lip made his father's face look ferocious.

"Yes, it hurts. But I'll beat up every paperhanger I see, till I've got no lips left at all."

Tyler's mother bent down to lay the iron pipe deep in the hole Tyler had dug for her. "You can't go on the air looking like that," she said.

"Genteel, that's what you are," said Tyler's father. "Bonnie just isn't. I took her to a music performance, an orchestra thing, and you know what she did? Clapped at all the wrong places. Clapped when nobody was supposed to clap. It was embarrassing. And I thought, Sherry would know when to clap."

Tyler's mother stood up. She had taken off her turban, and her hair hung loose around her shoulders and was plastered to her cheeks. "Shovel the dirt back in, Tyler." To Tyler's father she repeated, "You can't go on the air like that."

"I'm taking the evening off. Want to play?"

"Aw, Mom, go ahead," Tyler said.

"I don't think so," she said.

"We've known each other since the seventh grade, Sherry," said Tyler's father. "You won't come out and play with me?" He walked off whistling, slapping a hydrangea sprig into his palm.

Tyler and his mother spent the evening sitting on the porch eating fruitcake. Darkness gathered; fireflies blinked just above the grass.

"I wish you'd gone with him, Mom," Tyler said. He wished it with all his heart.

His mother fanned herself with the top of the fruitcake tin. "Ever since the seventh grade, he's been famous just for being handsome. Now, I think, he appreciates me. But I've fended him off with talk of another man."

"A married man," Tyler echoed.

"The love that hit so hard, in the cheese shop, has evaporated. To my surprise." She picked the nuts out of her third piece of cake. "I don't care about that paperhanger. Your father would have nothing to fear even if the paperhanger lived right next door. But now I've driven him back into the arms of Miss Heat Lightning. Honestly, Tyler, I feel so bad, I don't think I'll be able to do my laughing cure at all tomorrow morning."

"What's that sound?" Tyler said. They sat very still, listening.

They heard something coming up the driveway, something big, on hooves, loping, walking as if it had all the time in the world.

Tyler's father moved from the darkness into the yellow circle of light cast by the porch lamp. He was on his big white horse.

"Hey!" he called. "We jumped two fences on the way over here. And a parked car." He cantered in a circle, half-rising from the saddle. "Ya-hoo!"

Tyler's mother stood up so fast she knocked over her chair. She ran over to the horse and jumped on its back, clutching Tyler's father around the waist.

"Hold down the fort, son!" his father yelled.

"Bye, Tyler, honey," his mother called.

"Bye," said Tyler. He smiled at them as the horse galloped down the driveway, a pale rapid blur.

Later on, when the night was soft and total, he heard sounds coming from down the road, about a quarter mile away through the trees—music, laughter, car doors banging. He stood up and walked over to Massey's house.

There was Massey's mother, in a long purple skirt and a yellow blouse, and Massey's father, in jeans with a tuxedo jacket. The sleeves were too short. He had a plastic flower in his lapel. Their big shabby house was all lit up, with people pouring in and out of the doors, drinking beer in the yard, leaning against their cars. There were dozens of people—nobody Tyler knew—and lots of dogs. Paper lanterns hung from the elm trees.

"Tyler, my man," Massey greeted him. He tossed Tyler an orange. "Hope we ain't disturbing your sleep." He grinned. In the darkness his teeth were very white. His slanted green eyes shone.

"I don't want to sleep," Tyler said.

"Come over here," Massey said. They went to a long picnic table, covered in a big white sheet, holding fruit and cookies. But what commanded Tyler's attention was the sheet itself, hanging all the way to the dewy grass, catching the lantern light like a stage in the darkness. Moths fluttered there, dozens of them, pale green lunas and brown calico cecropias and little silvery ones whose name he didn't know. One was almost pink, one yellow, others sulfurous gold. Blue-black beetles whirred into the light, and a longlegs climbed delicately toward a dish of bananas.

"Mighty pretty," said Massey softly.

Tyler couldn't speak. He was too happy. At last he said, "Can I use your phone?" and Massey pointed toward the house.

Inside, a snake dance was going on, the column weaving and stomping through the halls, from the homely kitchen up the stairs and in every single room. The music was loud. Massey's mother saw him, swooped down, and kissed him; Massey's father thrust a bottle of beer into his hand. Tyler made his way to the telephone and called Susan.

"Hello?" she said sleepily, in her calm voice.

"Susan! It's Tyler. Susan, take a sheet out into your yard and shine a flashlight on it. You'll see something incredible—these beautiful bugs." He paused. "I'm at a wedding."

"Oh, Tyler," Susan said. Then for a long while she was silent. "Bugs?"

"Like a rainbow," said Tyler. "I love you."

Acknowledgments

The stories in this volume were previously published in the following publications: "The Belle Glade," *The Oxford American;* "Runaways," *The Greensboro Review;* "Rapture," in *Southern Humanities Review* as "The Rapture of the Deep"; "Doll," *Northwest Review;* "White Lilies," *The Virginia Quarterly Review;* "The Egg Man," *American Literary Review;* "Manna from the Sky," in *Four Quarters* as "Sweet Manna"; "The Girl Who Died in a Dance Marathon," *The Chattahoochee Review;* "Merry-Go-Sorry," *Alaska Quarterly Review;* "Mayflies," *Chelsea.*

The author wishes to express special thanks to the Tennessee Arts Commission, the Pennsylvania Council on the Arts, the Virginia Center for the Creative Arts, and the Corporation of Yaddo. All provided support and encouragement for the creation of this work of fiction.

About the Author

Photo by John Bensko

Cary Holladay is the winner of several literary prizes, including the O. Henry Short Story Contest and the *American Literary Review* fiction contest. She is the author of the acclaimed short-story collection *The People Down South.*